THE GIRL,
THE QUEEN,
AND THE CASTLE

D0066732

THE RHIANNA CHRONICLES

BOOK ONE: THE GIRL, THE DRAGON,
AND THE WILD MAGIC

BOOK TWO: THE GIRL, THE APPRENTICE,
AND THE DOGS OF IRON

BOOK THREE: THE GIRL, THE QUEEN,
AND THE CASTLE

THE GIRL, THE QUEEN, AND THE CASTLE

Book Three of The Rhianna Chronicles

Dave Luckett

SCHOLASTIC INC.

New York   Toronto   London   Auckland   Sydney
Mexico City   New Delhi   Hong Kong   Buenos Aires

To my sisters,
who know the meaning of family.

If you purchased this book without a cover, you should be aware that this book is stolen property. It was reported as "unsold and destroyed" to the publisher, and neither the author nor the publisher has received any payment for this "stripped book."

No part of this publication may be reproduced in whole or in part, or stored in a retrieval system, or transmitted in any form or by any means, electronic, mechanical, photocopying, recording, or otherwise, without written permission of the publisher. For information regarding permission, write to Permissions Department, Scholastic Australia, P.O. Box 579, Lindfield, New South Wales, Australia 2070.

ISBN 0-439-41189-0

Text copyright © 2002 by Dave Luckett.

Originally published in Australia in 2002 by Omnibus Books under the title *Rhianna and the Castle of Avalon*.
All rights reserved. Published by Scholastic Inc., 557 Broadway, New York, NY 10012, by arrangement with Omnibus Books, an imprint of Scholastic Australia.

SCHOLASTIC and associated logos are trademarks and/or registered trademarks of Scholastic Inc.

12 11 10 9 8 7 6 5 4 3 2   4 5 6 7 8 9/0
40

Printed in the U.S.A.
First American edition, June 2004

CHAPTER 1

Rhianna Wildwood woke. She didn't know why, at first. The night was as dark as a summer night could be, and it was short, already drawing to a close. In another hour the eastern sky would lighten and the day would begin. But not yet. It was still time to sleep.

She turned over in bed, but sleep was draining away. Something had woken her — a sound coming from the kitchen. She puzzled over it, sleepy and warm. For a moment she could not think what it was, but then she sat suddenly bolt upright. The sound was a glassy ringing like a fingernail striking a bowl, again and again. That was the spellcaster. Someone was calling.

At this time of night it must be important, and the caller could only be Magister Northstar. Spellcasters were made in pairs — and Magister Northstar had the twin to one in Rhianna's house. His spellcaster sat on his desk in his office, the Office of the Chancellor of

Wizardly College, in Avalon, a long day's sail across the water.

Rhianna threw off the covers and ran to the door of her room, but she was hardly there before her parents' door opened. Her father appeared in his nightshirt, tousled and bleary with sleep, but awake. He crossed to the dresser, where the spellcaster sat in its box. With a glance under his eyebrows at his daughter, he set it down on the table and opened it. The ringing sound became louder.

Rhianna's mother emerged, a taper in her hand. She went to the kitchen fire, found a live coal in the grate, lit the taper, and used it to light the big oil lamp. Yellow light flared up.

Loys Wildwood held the glass ball that was the spellcaster up to the lamp. The ringing stopped.

"Good morning to you, Magister," said Loys, wiping his hand over his face and staring down into the globe.

In the glass, a picture of Magister Northstar's study had appeared. It was a cluttered brown room, with stacks of paper on the desk, folders and files scattered about, and shelves and shelves of books. The papers were there because Magister Northstar was Chancellor of Wizardly College and the Mage on the Queen's Council; they had nothing to do with magic. He kept his magical gear in much better order than his College papers.

The picture turned around. Magister Northstar's face

appeared. He was just putting away the silver rod he had been striking the spellcaster with. He, too, was in his nightclothes. This must be important.

He looked tired, though that might have been because he had also been called from his sleep. He often said to Rhianna that he wasn't as young as he had been, and an old man needs his rest. In his dressing gown he looked even less impressive than usual. He was only a small man, a little round in the tummy, and his long white beard — his best feature — had not been brushed. It was only when you saw his eyes that you realized that this was a wizard, and someone to be careful of. His eyes were of a blue that darkened at the center like the sky, and they were just as deep.

"Good morning to you, Master Smith," he said politely, for Loys Wildwood was the blacksmith of the village of Smallhaven. Then he looked up briefly at his own candle, and his mouth turned down. "Though you can hardly say it's morning yet," he added. "I am sorry to have called at this time."

Mr. Wildwood smiled, still blinking. He stretched, tall in the flickering shadows of the lamplit kitchen, strong, square. "You'll be needing to talk to your apprentice, no doubt," he said, beckoning to Rhianna. "She's just here . . ."

"In a moment, Loys. I need to talk to you first." The

wizard ran a hand over his disordered hair, white like his beard. "Look, the Council has asked me to ask you . . . can Rhianna come over to Avalon for a while? With you and Mrs. Wildwood and whomever you will, of course. Something's come up."

Loys glanced at his wife and daughter. At that moment, his own apprentice, Eriseth Arwensgrove, looked in through the kitchen window from the outside. On warm summer nights she slept out in the meadow under a tree, after the way of her people, the Eldra. She would say that there was no need for a roof when you had the stars.

Mr. Wildwood invited her in with a wave of his hand. She opened the back door and stood silently in the doorway, leaning on her tall bow. "What sort of something?" he asked the Magister.

Northstar didn't answer the question directly. "Is Eriseth there?" he asked. "I would feel easier in my mind if she were to look around outside the house to make sure nobody else can hear this."

Mr. Wildwood looked a question at Eriseth. She nodded and slipped out again. The others made sure nobody was hiding, and Rhianna looked under her own bed.

Eriseth came in again as they finished, moving silent as starlight. She could do that, just as she could all but disappear from plain sight if she wanted to. It wasn't magic — Eriseth had none. The Eldra, the people of the forest, could all move like cats and shadows. She shook her head at Mr. Wildwood. Her bow was strung, Rhianna saw, and her arrows were in the quiver at her waist. It was just like Eriseth, Rhianna thought, to take all possible care. Eriseth had an arrow on the string, too, with an arrowhead that she had forged herself. Eriseth was the first of the Eldra to learn the craft of smithing, but she had taken to it like a bird to flight.

Mr. Wildwood returned her nod. "All right, Magister, no one else is listening," he said. "What's this all about?"

Magister Northstar sighed. Then his eyes rose and sought theirs. "Somebody has been making magic swords," he said softly. "Bespelling steel."

Rhianna felt a clutch at her heart. Suddenly, the warm night seemed colder. She glanced up at her father and saw the concern on his face. Cold iron was the opposite of magic. Only a person with a great gift would ever be able to make iron magical. Only a person with the Wild Magic — the kind of magic Rhianna had. And she had once done that very thing. She had thought she was the only one who could.

But now . . . now she was being told that there was somebody else. Rhianna's hand went to the jewel on the chain around her neck. It was rubies and gold, a necklace fit for a princess, and yet Rhianna Wildwood, a blacksmith's daughter from the outer islands, wore it.

"It's none of Rhianna's doing," said Loys Wildwood to the Magister. "I swear to it. She hasn't had that pendant off since you saw her last week. Or at all, other than when you knew. She can't work magic — especially so great a magic as that — while she wears it."

Magister Northstar's face didn't change. "I know that, Loys. Yet somebody has been making magical blades. At least one, and there may be more. The Council got the news this night. A Western Isles sea-thief called Byarni Ninefinger had one. He sacked two villages on the north coast of Avalon yesterday with two boatloads of raiders at his back, which is more than usual. They drove everyone out, killed anyone who faced them, stole everything they could fit into their longships, and burned the rest. Then they sailed away — or tried to. By luck, there was a Queen's ship on exercises just down the coast, and they saw the smoke. Even so, the raiders fought like fiends, calling out that they had magic on their side. And they did, in a sense."

"A sword, you said." Loys glanced at his wife and daughter. Rhianna moved closer to the spellcaster, and watched as the Magister's face became grim.

"Aye, a sword. It is not yet in my hands, for our ship

was badly damaged, and only made port this morning. We got the word by spellcaster, and the sword is being brought as fast as a horse can bring it. I should have it by tomorrow."

"They took the pirates, then."

"Yes. With heavy losses. But yes, they took them. And the sword as well. It is said to have been a burning brand — it burst into strange-colored flames as it was wielded. It could be a cheap trick, oil or some such . . ."

"But you don't think so."

"I know that Queen's shipmaster. He's no fool. If he says the sword is bespelled, that's enough for me, until I see for myself." Magister Northstar paused. His face looked out of the spellcaster at them, worried, furrowed. "If somebody has been making magical swords and selling them to the Western Islanders — or if they are making them for themselves — there'll be strife." He straightened. "I could tell you that the Queen herself commands your presence, and it would be true. She's as worried as the rest of us. But instead, Loys, I will ask. Please come as my honored guests, and bring Rhianna."

Mr. Wildwood's eyes sought his wife's face. Meg Wildwood was watching her daughter. Rhianna felt her heart thumping. Her hand came up of its own accord and touched the magical pendant at her throat.

It was there because she had the Wild Magic. Left to

itself, Rhianna's talent would take up all the magical power of the Land around her, becoming greater and greater, until she could not contain it. Then it would burst out like a river breaking a dam. The pendant drained the magic from her, and needed to be emptied from time to time, to return the power to the soil and the water of the Land from which it came. Uncontrolled, her power was dangerous.

Rhianna wished, just for a moment, that she could be like everyone else — a person with a little magic who could do ordinary everyday things with it, like find a lost pin or call fish into a net. But the Wild Magic was no quiet pony, to carry loads cheerfully. It was a stamping, snorting warhorse, strong and fast and fierce. She must not let it carry her away. She must not let others be trampled by it, either.

Rhianna nodded, and glanced across at Eriseth. They had faced a challenge like this before, and faced it together. Anyway, both knew that there was little choice. Both were apprentices, under oath to obey their masters. And Meg nodded also, to her husband.

Mr. Wildwood sighed softly. "All right, Magister. We'll come. All of us. As soon as may be. Give me a day to clear my work in the forge. Then I can spare a week, or two maybe, until the farmers start bringing in plowshares to be mended for the autumn plowing."

Northstar looked relieved. "Thank you. I'm sending a fast ship. It'll be there by dusk tonight." This *was* a hurry, and no mistake. "You can sail on the morning tide tomorrow." There was a knocking at the wizard's door. He sighed. "That'll be Odderer, with the summons to the Council meeting. I'll see you in a day or two. Good night — or good day — to you. And thank you."

The image in the glass faded and disappeared into silvery mist, which swirled and cleared. They were left staring at clear glass.

Mr. Wildwood put the spellcaster away and stood for a moment. Then he turned to his apprentice. "Well, Eris. No more sleep for us. If you can get the fire going, I'll be there in five minutes. We might as well start early and get it all out of the way." Eriseth nodded and slipped out silently, just as she always moved.

"I'll start packing," put in Mrs. Wildwood. "You'll have to help me, Rhianna. Loys, how long do you think . . . ?"

Mr. Wildwood's mouth turned down. "As long as it takes, I suppose. At the very least, until they're sure it isn't Rhianna. And, after that, as long as they want. The Magister was asking, you know, but he might just as well have been ordering." His face softened, and took on his usual cheerfulness. "But just think. We're going to be Northstar's honored guests in the Palace. We could have a worse sort of holiday."

He went to dress in his working clothes. Mrs. Wildwood sat and began writing out lists of things to take, but Rhianna stood where she was, her hand still touching her magical pendant, frowning. She knew that nobody really wanted to do this. Nor did she.

Smallhaven was their home, and there was no saying how long it might be before they saw it again. Avalon was the great city across the water, on the Home Island that was also called Avalon. It was a very different place from the small village where she had lived for as long as she could remember.

More worrying, the Wild Magic was loose in the world. It had carried away whoever had it, and it had already trampled people underfoot. It had destroyed them with fire and the sword. Rhianna wondered if she could stop it before the whole world went up in flames.

CHAPTER 2

It was as Magister Northstar had said. The Wildwoods and Eriseth were treated as honored guests. They went aboard a Queen's ship at sunset that very day, to sail by the following morning's tide. In the last of the long day's light, Rhianna and Eriseth looked over the rail at the village that was their home.

Smallhaven was a single street — with shops, the forge, and an inn — running up the slope away from the seafront. Behind it were the fields, and beyond them a range of hills. Rhianna glanced at Eriseth's face. Eris was watching the hills. Beyond them again were the lands of the Eldra, the forests that were home to her people, and then the mountains that were home to stranger folk still — trolls and giants and dragons. Rhianna could attest to the dragons. She had seen one for herself. But Eriseth's face showed she wasn't thinking about dragons.

"Are you sorry to be leaving, Eris?" asked Rhianna.

Eriseth kept her eyes on the distant range. She shrugged one shoulder, as if to say that she was both unsure and unsure of why she was unsure. "I shouldn't be," she replied, after a moment. "I have left my home before this. And yet . . ." Her eyes fell to the houses and the quiet street of the little village. "And yet, you know, I *am* sorry to leave. Smallhaven seemed so, well, quiet and calm. Like home. But Avalon won't be like home at all. I hear it's a lot bigger, with buildings everywhere."

Rhianna nodded. She hooked her arm through Eriseth's as they stood at the rail. "It isn't like home for any of us." She glanced at the center hatchway of the ship. Her father had just emerged from it. "But home, you know, is people, not things."

Mr. Wildwood crossed the deck and stood behind them, putting a hand on each girl's shoulder. He seemed determined to be cheerful. "They've been very good to us. The shipmaster and his mate have given us their cabins for the night. They'll sleep ashore and leave with the morning tide, well before dawn, while we're still asleep. The weather looks set fair. Just think, when you wake up tomorrow, you'll be out at sea, and we'll reach Avalon by tomorrow evening."

The girls nodded. Eriseth glanced up at her master, then returned to watching the village, knowing that he was doing the same, looking like a man storing up the warmth of a fire before going out on a cold day.

They went early to bed, slept only a little, and were all on deck before dawn to watch the few lights of Smallhaven recede into the darkness. As they watched, gray streaks grew in the sky. Soon they were able to make out first the line of the hills against the fading stars, and then the loom of the headland. They reached the harbor mouth, and the wide ocean stretched before them. At almost the same moment, the sun blinked across the blue water and it was bright day. The ship heeled to the breath of the true trade wind. The sailors trimmed the sail to it, and the ship swooped like a gull. She dug her sharp bows into a roller, sending foam flying. After that, it was hard to be downcast.

But Rhianna still glanced back towards her home, the outline of its hills now dim in the distance, before she went to watch the dolphins playing around the bows.

It was a quick passage. The wind was a good one, a brisk nor'wester that served equally well going or coming from Avalon to Smallhaven. The land dropped below the world's edge behind them, but it was not long before another land rose up out of the marching sea ahead. It was flatter and more rounded than Smallhaven's island, with

13

a hint of checkered fields even at the first sight of it. Avalon.

A vague cloud fretted on the wind there, the smoke of a thousand chimneys and forges and mills. That was the smoke of Avalon the City, the home of Magister Northstar and the wizards of Wizardly College — and of the Queen, Her Majesty Gloriana the Second.

They came into harbor in the last light, the city almost golden in the low sun — Avalon was built of honey-colored stone. A rowing-galley took them in tow, and the sailors went aloft to strike down the topmast.

Rhianna stared over the rail. Where Smallhaven had boasted a single wooden pier, here there were a dozen stone-built quays, a long, solid stone harbor wall, and a basin crowded with ships from the Western Isles and even from Glasheel and Altermar, far to the south and the east. All loading and unloading, all bustle and movement. But the galley, with the ship in tow, headed for none of the merchant docks. Rhianna watched them slide past, one after the other. When they passed the last dock, she realized that they were making for tall water-gates with a great portcullis that was being raised even now. A stone wall bulked up on either side of it. It cut off an inner, private part of the harbor.

They rowed under the gate, into the quiet water beyond. Now Rhianna realized why the tall mast had been brought down — it was so that the ship would fit under the gate. Thinking that, she looked up — and gaped.

Above her loomed Avalon Castle. They had come into the pool that contained its private landing dock. Here was the Queen's own yacht, tall and stately, and a stone quay to tie up at. Beyond the dock was a landing-stage, then a great sweeping stone stair — and then the Castle itself.

Unlike the buildings of the port, it was a massive, gaunt pile, with tiny slits instead of windows, and tall blank walls. It faced out over the harbor from its height, watching over the busy town and the anchorage, and the twinkle of steel reflected from its battlements, high above.

Eriseth nudged Rhianna and pointed. A small crowd was gathering at the quay, but it was a crowd that looked quite different from the varied, bustling throng on the harbor docks. These people were still and ordered, and dressed in rich, strong colors — moss green and crimson, deep blue and old gold. Around them, lining the dock, stood two files of soldiers in polished breastplates and helmets, wearing green cloaks and bearing silver-headed spears and bright enameled shields. The device on the shields was that of the Queen herself: three golden apples on a green field. More soldiers lined the stairs up to the great gate of Avalon Castle.

"The Queen's Guard," said her mother, who was

standing to look over Rhianna's shoulder. Meg Wildwood was born in Avalon, and knew the city well. "They turn out to welcome important visitors. I wonder who's arriving?"

Loys Wildwood looked about, and saw the deference on the faces of the seamen, and that no other ship was moving in the enclosed pool around them. Already the portcullis was dropping back into place. "Don't look now, love, and be glad you're wearing your best gown," he said. "Because I think it's us."

Rhianna had already had the same thought. The ship was coming into the dock, and the faces in the crowd were becoming clear. The man at the head was Magister Northstar, in ceremonial robes of gold and black, his tall hat on his head, his staff in his hand. And that would mean that the group behind him was the Conclave of Wizardly College, the magical scholars whose work was to find and record new spells, to harness magic for the good of the land and the people. They stood in their ranks, the apprentices behind, the master mages at the front in their robes and gowns, to welcome their guest. Rhianna blinked and gulped. Honored, indeed.

Ropes were thrown across, the ship tied up at the quay, and a bridge was hauled up to the side. The sailors formed two lines, and the Wildwoods disembarked between them in style. Mr. and Mrs. Wildwood exchanged glances, and then nudged Rhianna ahead of them to go down the gangway first. It seemed that all this fuss was really for her. She reached the bottom of the ramp and bowed to her master, as was proper. Rhianna was Magister Northstar's only apprentice, and she owed him formal respect.

But the Magister took her hand and raised her up, and then nodded to her parents. "Welcome," he said, and he sounded as if he meant it. "Thrice welcome."

Mr. and Mrs. Wildwood nodded back. It was difficult to be formal with the Magister, who'd been in their house many a time, but this was the first time they had seen him in such robes, with his fellow mages behind him. He looked impressive, and the ranks of wizards be hind him almost more impressive still, for he was their Head and the Chancellor of their College, and could command their presence, the most powerful wizards of the Realm. Some of them didn't look too pleased about it, either. Rhianna felt shy of him for the first time since they had met.

But he was already turning to another man beside him. Rhianna had hardly noticed him, for this was no wizard, but a small, slight man with a foxy face and russet hair, dressed in the green of the Queen's livery.

"May I present . . . Master Longacre, the Queen's Chamberlain. Master Wildwood, Mrs. Wildwood. Miss

Wildwood. And Eriseth Arwensgrove of the Eldra, who comes as the representative of her people."

Master Longacre bowed gracefully to them all in turn. "A great pleasure, sir, my ladies. I come from Her Majesty the Queen, who commands your presence at supper this evening."

Mr. Wildwood glanced at his wife, who was pink with embarrassment. "Ah . . . we will, of course, obey the Queen's command . . . but, well, I'm not sure . . . that is, that we have suitable . . ."

The Chamberlain smiled. "Her Majesty asked me to say that it will be quite a small gathering, and not formal. Court dress will not be necessary — indeed, what you are wearing is perfectly suitable. Her Majesty knows that you have come in haste, at the request of the Magister, and her own."

Mrs. Wildwood looked relieved. But Magister Northstar was already turning again. "May I present . . ." he began.

Rhianna watched him as he introduced the senior wizards of the College. There was the Bursar and the Master and the Librarian, the Wardens of the Fire, the Water, the Wind, and the Stone, the Senior Spellmaker, the Professors of Chant and of Sign, of Hand and of Word and of Rune, and many others. Her head was spinning long before they were done, and the faces were only a blur in her mind.

Her head was still spinning as she climbed the steps, following the Magister, with her parents and Eriseth behind. To left and right the soldiers stood like statues in their armor with the Queen's sign on their shields. Above her the walls of the castle loomed, torches on the battlements making a line of light.

After the grand gate of the castle, there was a small yard, a winding stair, then a hall through which they hurried, and beyond that a small square chamber. The chamber had two doors — one they entered through, and another on the opposite side. Two more soldiers, the same as the ones below, stood guard on either side of that door.

Master Longacre bowed again and opened the door. Beyond was a large room, the walls paneled with dark wood, but bright with the light of many wax candles. A table was already set out along the length of the room. Supper came in at once, brought in covered dishes by silent servants. They were not the only guests, Rhianna could see. Probably the Queen had many people to feed, and there were others taking supper there at the same time. None was as gorgeously dressed as Magister Northstar, though.

He glanced down at his heavy, rich robes with a grimace, and spoke to Mr. Wildwood. "If you don't mind, Loys, I'll just leave you here for ten minutes while I change out of this getup. Then I can eat my supper in comfort. Master Longacre will look after you." He nodded to the Chamberlain and left through a small door that Rhianna hadn't noticed before. Master Longacre beckoned to a servant, and chairs were pulled out at the table. The Wildwoods took their seats, with Rhianna resolving to mind her manners.

She wondered where the Queen was. She looked around, but there was nobody wearing a crown. Well, of course the Queen would hardly eat with ordinary people. And they did all look quite ordinary. They sat at one long table, and at its head sat an older man with a black-and-grey beard, a merchant by his dress, and six or seven younger ones — apparently soldiers out of uniform, for they wore swords and seemed hard and composed. There was also a young woman sitting to the right of the merchant, dark-haired, in a plain blue gown and overdress, and another, a girl still in her teens, freckled and slim, with her hair, a shade lighter than the other's, worn in a plait. There was enough likeness in their faces for Rhianna to think that they might be sisters. Rhianna nodded at them politely, and received smiles and a nod in return. She turned to her food.

Rhianna hardly remembered that supper later. She

was hungry after the long day and the journey, and the food was welcome. There was a roast carved for her by a special servant who did nothing else, wonderful light bread and fresh greens — and a dessert of summer fruits and cream. But she was being so careful about her manners that she had little time to spare for anything else.

Halfway through the meal, Northstar returned, still with his staff in his hand — for he was never without it — but in his ordinary robe, a dark blue one, a little frayed at the hem. Nor was he wearing his tall hat indoors, and so he looked quite ordinary, too, like the rest of them. He, too, nodded at the young lady in the blue dress and the others before he sat and broke his bread.

"A little wine, if you please," he said to the serving man. "Ah. Thank you. It's been a long day." He spooned up soup. "How is the Queen?" he asked Rhianna. "She looks a little worried."

"The Queen?" asked Rhianna. "I haven't met her yet. I suppose they might take us to see her when we've finished supper."

The wizard paused, a piece of bread halfway to his mouth. He stared a moment at Rhianna, and then put the bread down again. He opened his mouth and closed it again. "Didn't Master Longacre tell you?" he asked.

Master Longacre leaned across. "Her Majesty gave instructions that the formalities are to wait until after the meal. She remarked that it would be discourteous to make hungry people wait on her convenience, especially since they had come so far and fast at her request. But, since you have finished, I'll present you now. Mr. Wildwood, Mrs. Wildwood, Miss Arwensgrove? If you'll follow me?"

Rhianna rose, expecting to be led through the door and into some vast room where a grand lady sat on a gold throne, all robed in velvet and ermine, a scepter in her hand, a crown on her head. But the Chamberlain simply crossed the floor, the Wildwoods and Eriseth trailing behind, and stopped behind the young lady in the blue dress. She turned with a smile. The younger girl also swung around, and the man with the pepper-and-salt beard put down his knife and nodded.

"Your Majesty, Your Royal Highness, Your Grace, may I present . . ." began Master Longacre, and Rhianna realized with a shock that he was talking to the young lady in blue.

Master Longacre was going through their names, one at a time. Her father was bowing, her mother curtsying. Eriseth nodded, as she would to the Wisewoman of her Grove — the Eldra had no kings or queens.

". . . Rhianna Wildwood, apprentice to Magister Northstar, Your Majesty." Master Longacre looked down at her, and Rhianna made a jerky curtsy, still in shock.

But the young lady in blue only smiled. "Rhianna, a

pleasure. I do hope you'll enjoy your stay. This is my sister, Serena, and my uncle, Duke Robert of Lamortin." The younger girl and the man in the merchant's clothes nodded and smiled. Rhianna curtsied again, doubting her ears. That would be Her Royal Highness the Princess Serena Therese, and His Grace the Duke of Lamortin, who commanded the Queen's ships and her army, too. The shock was only getting worse. There was a roaring in Rhianna's ears.

But there was a hand on her shoulder, and the Queen's eyes rose. Magister Northstar stood behind his apprentice, straightening up after his bow. The Queen smiled. "And here is one who needs no introduction. Welcome, Antheus. Have you any more to tell us about this sword?"

Real friendliness was in the Queen's voice, thought Rhianna, and she used Northstar's first name as if she always used it. And she had a nice smile. Rhianna began to like her.

But the wizard shook his head. "It arrived just this afternoon, Your Majesty. I have had the first tests conducted, and indeed it is magical. The College Council is working on it now, and we shall meet before the evening is out. I hope to have news before you retire."

Gloriana's face became intent. "I shall not be retiring until I hear, Antheus. Send to me as soon as you know."

"I shall, Your Majesty. We'll be getting on with it at once, if we may be excused."

"Of course. We shall be pleased to see you again at court, all of you. Good evening."

Then it was simply a matter of bowing again and backing away, for you do not turn your back on the Queen. Master Longacre ushered them out. Northstar turned, once they had left the dining room.

"I must get back to the College, to see what else they have found out. I'll come and collect Rhianna as soon as we know anything. I'm sorry, but it looks like it will be a late night — and it was an early morning, too. I'm sure that Master Longacre will make you comfortable." He nodded and departed. Clearly there was a great deal on his mind, for he forgot to smile.

"We put you in rooms in the west wing, near to Wizardly College, but up two floors. I've had your things taken there," said Master Longacre. "This way, if you please." He showed them out, and they followed him.

Rhianna said nothing. She was looking around as she walked, and realizing that the Castle of Avalon went on a long way farther than she thought. Some of the passageways were grand and stately, with carpets and wall hangings rich with crimson and gold thread. But as they went, more bare floors appeared. Some were stone, and some wooden. Some felt like they were part of the earth itself, old, firm, not echoing, while others sprung underfoot. It was a long way with many turnings along corridors and passages, through rooms, and up and down small stairs, so that it was difficult to say what floor you were on.

"I don't think I could find my way out again," said Mr. Wildwood after a while, looking about him.

The Chamberlain smiled. "It *is* difficult. Quite a maze, in fact. The Castle started out as a hollow square of walls, but the square got filled in with buildings, and then it partly burned down, not once but at least twice. Over time, it just grew. More towers and galleries and wings were added and another ring wall built. But there was always a need for more space — Wizardly College, for one thing, but also workshops for the Navy, storerooms for a siege, headquarters for the army, stables and offices, apartments for visiting royalty and nobles . . . and other distinguished guests." He somehow managed to bow as he walked. "It just grew and grew. And then parts of it became outmoded, or not needed anymore, and so they were knocked down, walled up, or built over, or simply not used. Like this." He gestured.

They were marching along a corridor, but the left-hand wall came to an end suddenly, and they found themselves looking down over a rail into an enormous empty room, its polished wooden floor winking up at them in dim candlelight. The far wall was almost out of sight.

They were in a gallery, two tall men's height above the floor.

"That's King Herold's ballroom," said Master Longacre. "We stand in the musicians' gallery. They were very fond of dancing, three hundred years ago."

"It looks . . . sad, all dark like this," remarked Rhianna without thinking. A moment later she was biting her lip. What a rude thing to say!

But Master Longacre simply nodded, looking sad himself. "It does indeed seem a little forlorn. There hasn't been a court ball in years. Her Majesty liked to dance, too, and Her Highness the Princess also."

"Why don't they, then?" asked Mrs. Wildwood, who also liked to dance. "Surely they can hold a dance if they want to?"

Master Longacre made a graceful gesture and they walked on. "Well . . . a court ball isn't just a dance, you know. It's sort of a State occasion. Her Majesty can't invite only the people she likes, just because she likes them. All the foreign ambassadors come, and there's always a lot of politics and statecraft and jockeying for position. And then there are the suitors for the Queen's hand. And for her sister the Princess's, too, lately."

"Suitors?" asked Mrs. Wildwood.

Master Longacre gave a weary smile. "Yes. Her Majesty is young and unmarried. Whomever she marries will be the Prince Consort, and a very important man. Of course, the Queen would still rule, but her husband would have great influence. Many noble families, and foreign royal houses, too, desire to make such a match, and all send their sons to court here. There's a lot of jealousy and rivalry, and young gallants sighing and flattering and fighting duels and writing bad verse about the Queen or the Princess. Fortunately, Her Majesty has a very level head on her shoulders."

"She doesn't like any of them, then?" asked Eriseth, puzzled. The Eldra, her people, didn't marry for life — and she still found the idea a little odd.

"Oh, they're all very pleasant, I'm sure. But marrying this one or that would give power and prestige to one family or another, and that might not be such a good thing. Marrying a foreign prince would give his people a say over our affairs, and that might be even worse. There were stories . . ." Master Longacre broke off suddenly, as if he felt he had said too much.

Rhianna liked stories. "What stories?" she asked, and her parents glanced at each other. Her father cleared his throat.

But Master Longacre simply smiled again. "Oh, it was said that the young Captain of the Guard, Lysandus of Redhill, had gained the Queen's favor. He might have been a possibility, but . . . oh, matters seem to have cooled off. Something about the way he treated a horse that shied while he was riding with the Queen. Her Majesty cannot abide cruelty to animals. Personally, I never thought there was anything in the rumor at all. Lysandus is a likeable enough young fellow, with big broad shoulders, but there's never a thought in his head. Ah. We're here. These are your rooms."

There was a paneled door off the corridor, and Master Longacre opened it with a flourish. Warm light spilled out.

The rooms were cheerful and quiet, two bedrooms and a sitting room paneled in wood the color of old honey. A window looked out over a small courtyard garden with a fountain in its center. It was a pretty garden, but it was enclosed by other tall walls, with other windows looking down. The two chests they had brought from Smallhaven were being unpacked by silent Palace servants and the clothes and things put away. It took only a few minutes. Then the servants bowed and left as quietly as they had worked.

The Wildwoods stood and looked at each other.

CHAPTER 3

It was long past Rhianna's usual bedtime when Northstar's knock finally came on the door. Eriseth had gone to bed — well, to sleep, anyway. She was rolled in a blanket on the floor in the smaller of the two bedrooms, the window open as wide as it would go, so that she could see the stars. Rhianna lolled on a couch in the sitting room, half asleep herself, reading a book on spellcasting that she had brought from home, and trying to concentrate. Her parents sat in chairs, Mrs. Wildwood sewing, Mr. Wildwood fidgeting. Every now and again he would get up and take a turn around the room, moving restlessly, his fingers twitching behind his back.

When the knock came, he hurried to the door and opened it. Northstar looked in, unsmiling. "We're ready to go to the Queen, Loys. I think it would be useful to have Rhianna's insight. Nobody else in the College has the slightest idea of how to bespell iron, and anything she can tell us will help."

Mr. Wildwood hesitated. "It's late, Magister."

The wizard nodded. "I know. But the Queen's business brooks no delays. Will you come, too?"

Her father glanced across at Rhianna. She had risen and put the book down, and now she came forward. Mr. Wildwood sighed and stood aside, following her out.

They walked with Magister Northstar. Again, Rhianna lost track of the turns and the corners within minutes, and again she was surprised when the last door opened before her.

It was not at all what she had expected for a Queen's Council chamber — merely a small room with a worn carpet over a stone floor. A table, old, dark, and solid, stood in the middle, among stiff wooden chairs with worn red velvet cushions on their seats and arms. In the chair at the head of the table sat Queen Gloriana of Avalon, wearing the same ordinary blue dress as before, one elbow on her chair-arm, resting her head on her hand. There were shadows under her eyes, but those eyes were bright and watchful.

On the table in front of her lay a long, heavy sword with a silvery blade, its hilt towards her. It was elaborate and rich with gilding, the pommel picked out with bright gems. More gold glittered on the blade, but its edges were dark, brownish, as if smeared with burnt butter. Rhianna glanced at it, and tiny cat's claws prickled up her back. Magic was there, the Wild Magic. She knew it well . . . and yet at the same time it was strange, sharp, new. All the Wild Magic she had seen before was her own. This was not.

Magister Northstar saw her start. "Wild Magic?" he asked quietly, and she nodded. "What else can you tell me about it?"

Rhianna stared at the sword. "It's . . . strange. There's a feeling about it." She groped for words. At last she said, "It tastes of fear, and unwillingness, and sorrow." She shook her head and looked up at him, and her master nodded slowly.

Standing stiffly behind the Queen's chair was a blond young man in the green uniform of the Queen's Guard, with loops of gold braid on his shoulders. He had glanced sharply at Rhianna and her father as they had entered. Another tap sounded at the door. It opened, and another man in a wizard's robe entered. He was younger, narrow-faced, with thinning brown hair. Unlike most wizards, he was clean-shaven. His staff was a rich golden-hued maple wood.

Rhianna looked around at the last arrival. It seemed

to her that she had seen his face before. Magister Northstar confirmed it. This man had been standing on the dock to meet them.

"Your Majesty," he said, "I believe you know Master Odderer, Registrar of Wizardly College. I have asked him to come because he was the one who found the sword's release word."

Lord Odderer bowed. "A simple matter, Your Majesty," he smiled. "No more than the word for fire in the Western tongue. I can't think why nobody else tried it."

His voice was smooth and rich. Just like his clothes, thought Rhianna. He was wearing the full formal robes of a wizard, and in them he looked more impressive than Magister Northstar. He was taller by a head, for a start. If you were to go by his clothes, thought Rhianna, you'd say he was the most important person here.

But then the Queen spoke, and as soon as you heard her voice, you knew who was important and who wasn't. "Welcome, Master, and thank you for your efforts," she said. "And now let us see what we have here."

She nodded to the young man in uniform behind her. "Captain Lysandus, if you please. Be careful with it. Hold it well away from you. The word, sir, if you would be so good."

The Captain leaned over and picked up the sword by its fancy hilt. Rhianna remembered where she had heard his name before, and indeed the Queen seemed cold and formal when she spoke to him. He held the weapon point-upright at arm's length, his muscles bunching with the effort.

Lord Odderer stepped back. *"Surt!"* he called.

For a moment, there was a rising smell of hot, sharp brimstone. Rhianna recoiled, nose wrinkling, eyes watering. Curls of greasy smoke arose from the upright blade. Then, with a *woof!*, as if it had blown a great breath out, the sword blade burst into candle-yellow flame. It was smoky, sooty fire, stinking of magic, green at its core, dribbling flames in droplets and spurts onto the old carpet. The soldier stamped on them, shaking the sword, and more fell down. The blade flared, roaring in the draft, making the candlelight look pale. The flames reached almost to the ceiling, which was beginning to blacken and smoke.

"Enough!" called Magister Northstar. "The word of cancellation, Registrar."

But Lord Odderer was staring into the flame, fascinated, his face lined with the unhealthy light. Magister Northstar had to tug at his robe. "The word!" he demanded.

The other shook his head, as if collecting his thoughts. *"Utt,"* he said, in a quiet, conversational sort of voice.

The flame sputtered and died down. A few ripples of

fire ran up the blade, flickered, and went out with a pop. The sword was as it had been — a golden-hilted, gemmed, silvery-gray blade with edges stained with soot.

The Captain stamped out the last of the flames smoldering on the carpet. He lowered the sword and then held it by the hilt, point on the floor.

The Queen turned to Magister Northstar. "Magic indeed, and no trick?" she asked calmly, without expression.

The Magister cleared his throat. "Magic it is, Majesty. The Wild Magic, as my apprentice has just informed me."

Queen Gloriana sat down again, upright in her chair. "Then what remains is to find where it came from and who made it." Her face was calm, and the words cool and clear. "We will do whatever it takes to stop them."

There was a short silence. Then Lord Odderer cleared his throat. "As to who made it, Your Majesty, I beg to point out that only one person has ever been known to bespell iron." He seemed troubled, but determined to canvass an unpleasant truth. His voice was hesitant. "Indeed, we have only just recently been told of her abilities, as a great State secret."

Magister Northstar's brows drew down like the white outriders of a snowstorm. "What exactly do you mean, Lord Odderer?" he asked.

The other put up a hand. "I know, I know. It's a most

unpleasant thing to have to say. Nevertheless, we must consider all the possibilities, and really, Magister, how many mages *could* have done it? For a thousand years we have thought that putting spells on iron was impossible. Now we're told that two people who could do it have popped up in a single season. Is that likely? And this lass is, I'm told, a blacksmith's child. I would imagine that she's had plenty of contact with iron. Where better to learn how to work magic on it, and where better to obtain weapons to bespell?" He made a helpless little gesture. "Forgive me, Magister, but you must know it's my duty sometimes to tell you things that you don't want to hear. There are wild tales circulating."

Rhianna heard a roaring in her ears. The worst of it was that there was reason behind the words. She had indeed bespelled iron once, in a fit of temper, and dreadful things had come of it. She looked up to her master in appeal.

Magister Northstar's voice was cold. "If you accuse my apprentice of abusing her talent, Registrar, you also accuse me of carelessness in her training. I tell you it is not so."

The Registrar nodded, and wet his lips. The Queen's eyes were on him, and in those eyes was a warning that even Rhianna could read, but he spoke on regardless, stubbornly. "I'm sure that you believe her to be innocent,

Magister, but you haven't been able to watch her every moment. Can anyone expect that a mere child — and from the laboring classes, too — would understand how dangerous a Wild Talent can be? I'm sure . . ."

"You're sure of a great many things, Wizard. Too many."

That wasn't Magister Northstar's voice, nor yet the Queen's. It was Loys Wildwood who spoke. His voice was calm and cool, but there was anger in its depths.

Master Odderer raised one eyebrow. "I've no doubt you understand iron, sir. It's your trade. But I understand magic, and I tell you that a mage who can use magic on iron is unheard of. Unheard of until your daughter did it, that is. The last Wild Talent appeared over forty years ago, and he was simple, it seems. To find the last one with all their wits, you'd have to go back nearly a thousand. Who else could have done this? And it is, of course, true that magic swords would sell for a much higher price than ordinary smith's work."

Loys turned pale, and Rhianna felt his hand on her shoulder clench. He drew in breath, but what he was going to say was never heard, and that was probably just as well. Magister Northstar got in first.

"Enough!" he said, and his voice was flat. "The Wildwoods are my guests, and I give my word that it is not my apprentice nor Master Wildwood who has done this."

"But, Magister . . ."

But the Registrar was overridden by a quiet voice with even more authority. The Queen had risen. "Master Registrar, it seems to me that you do little credit to your own office, to dispute with your Chancellor over such a matter. He has given his bond on it, and I hold that to be good. You will not raise this again, on pain of my displeasure."

The Registrar lowered his head stiffly, like a puppet. "I ask Your Majesty's pardon, and that of the Magister . . . and of the young lady and her father. I meant no offense. I said what I believed had to be said. But of course the Magister's word is the final one on the matter. I would never dream of disputing it."

The Queen nodded. "Is there anything else that you can tell me about this sword?" she asked, at large. The wizards shook their heads. "Then perhaps we should sleep on this and begin again in the morning."

Loys Wildwood cleared his throat. "Begging your pardon, ma'am, but as this Lord said, it is my trade to know iron. Perhaps I might be able to tell you a little about this thing." He jerked a thumb at the sword, still in the hands of the Captain. "There's something strange about it."

Queen Gloriana stared at him a moment. "Of course, Master Smith," she said. "Forgive me. I must be tired. Who better to know steel? Captain, please give the sword to Mr. Wildwood."

For a moment, it seemed as though the soldier would protest. He turned his head towards the Queen and his mouth opened. Her Majesty glanced at him, once, coldly. He jerked his head and handed the sword across the table, hilt-first, his gloved hands on the blade.

Loys Wildwood took it from him, hefting it easily, and ran his own hands over the hilt. He rubbed the gilded cross-guard, sniffed disdainfully, and inspected the pommel, pushing a thick thumbnail against the inset gems. Then he looked more closely still at the long, heavy blade, rubbing the soot off it with the ball of his thumb.

He nodded once. He lowered the sword, put the point on the stone floor, and held the hilt in his left hand. Before anyone could say anything, he placed his right knee in the middle of the flat of the blade and pulled the hilt sharply towards him, pressing down with the knee. The sword gave a metal groan and bent like a green twig.

Everyone drew in a breath. Magister Northstar opened his mouth, but the Captain got in first. "Sir!" he barked, and he started around the table towards Mr. Wildwood.

But the big smith simply grunted as if he had seen what he expected to see, and held the sword up. The blade had stayed bent like a bow. He showed it to the soldier, and a grim smile was on his lips. "A strange sort of sword, staying bent like that. A blade should spring back from a blow, don't you think, Captain? But this is soft metal. Look" — he tested the edge with a finger — "feel the nicks in it. It's already blunt, and it's only been used once."

The Captain stared at the sword. It looked silly now, with its bright gems, golden hilt, and bent blade. "And," Mr. Wildwood went on, "the cross-guard is wrought iron, not steel. It would break like a pot if it were hit hard. Pity about the hand holding the hilt, when that happened. The welding on the pommel is poorly done — just look at those clumsy hammer marks. The claws holding the gems are copper. Already they're showing green. The gilding — why, it's only gold leaf. I can scrape it off with my nail. I'm no jeweler, but I'll bet my forge the gems are glass."

His face showed his contempt. "It's a cheat, a piece of rubbish tricked up to look expensive. Whoever made it ought to be ashamed. This is not work for a decent smith. Anyone who says that I made it, or could make it, doesn't know me. I'd rather my hands lost their cunning than send such a thing out of my shop." He leaned the sword against the table and dusted his hands, as if to wipe its touch away.

There was a short silence in the room. Magister Northstar broke it. "But," he said slowly, "that would mean that the pirate who had the blade did not make it himself, nor did he get it from anyone who wished him well. Surely such a person would give him a good sword, one that was well made, magical or no."

Loys Wildwood nodded. "Indeed, Magister. This Byarni Ninefinger, the pirate, was cheated. I hope he didn't pay too much for it."

"All that he had, Loys. All that he had."

"Perhaps we are reading too much into this." The voice belonged to Registrar Odderer. "Quite likely the person who made the blade was simply not a swordsmith. One would hardly expect so powerful a magic user to concern himself — or herself — with manual labor."

Mr. Wildwood snorted. "No. Whoever made this made it to deceive, and made it that way by intent. The work is cheap and shoddy, not simply unskilled." He had not looked at the Registrar. Rhianna did, and her face was tight with anger. *Manual labor*, indeed! Why, she ought to . . .

But her father's grip was hard on her shoulder. *Keep your temper*, he was saying. She sighed. He was right. Bad things happened when she lost it.

The Queen had noticed, though. "Thank you, Master Wildwood. It is good to have the word of one who has your skills. Magic, as we all know, isn't everything, and other trades are just as honored in our sight."

She glanced at the Registrar. Lord Odderer stiffened, but he kept silence.

"So then," she went on, "what do we know?" She stared around at them. "Can anyone say where this cheap trick came from?"

"If you'll allow, Your Majesty," said Mr. Wildwood, "I can tell you it was never made in the Western Isles. They've no use for poor smithing there, and they'd use lines of twisty knotwork to decorate a sword, not swirls like these. I've seen Glasheel work that looks like this, but if they'd made the blade, it'd be curved. No. I've a notion that it was made in this realm, and likely here in Avalon."

The Captain twitched, as if stung. He spoke for the first time. "Here? One of the Queen's subjects made this to sell to a pirate?" he asked. "Your Majesty, that sounds far-fetched. We would surely have heard of such a plot."

Loys Wildwood said nothing. He folded his arms and stood back.

"Thank you, Master Smith." The Queen turned a sharp eye on the soldier. "I doubt, Captain, that we know every would-be profiteer and dubious merchant in Avalon," she said. "Or every mage, either." She looked at Northstar. "A traitor, then, Antheus."

The Magister's face was grim. "It would seem so, Your

Majesty. It fits. The Western Islanders have some war-locks and witches, but no proper College of Magic, and little chance for study of the Art. I doubt if they *could* make such a thing, even if a Wild Talent were to arise among them. And, as the Master Smith has shown us, it certainly wasn't made by someone who wanted to *help* this pirate. It was made simply for profit, by someone who cared about nothing else. There are such people in Avalon, as elsewhere."

"Then we must find this person, Antheus. And soon. In a way, it is well that it is one of our own subjects. At least they are within our reach. Captain . . ."

Captain Lysandus shook his head. "A traitor? As the Registrar asks, are we not reading too much into this? Must we search for treason, and must your guards be ac-cused of laxness, on the word of a village blacksmith? I say we look to King Hrothwil of the Western Isles for this. It is time that a little fire was sent to him in return. Majesty, let me . . ."

"No. I have had enough of this constant urge to battle, Captain. You are too fond of it, as I have told you before."

Lysandus's face was bitter. "Better to have war with the outlanders than to see treason among your own, Gloriana."

The Queen rose. Her face was as white as a snow-storm, and her voice as cold. "You forget yourself. There is now nothing between us that allows you the use of our personal name. You made petition for leave a week ago. It is granted, Captain. Return when you are once again able to serve us as we require. You may go."

For a moment, Lysandus stood there, eyes blazing, as if he would disobey the Queen's command. His mouth opened to say something more, but then it closed, and his face closed with it. He bowed with a choppy jerk of the head, then backed away and turned on his heel to pass through the door.

Queen Gloriana turned to the others. "I find I must lay the task on you, Antheus — and on you, Master Wildwood. You both have the wisdom of your different callings, and more beside. Find me this traitor."

Magister Northstar bowed. They all bowed. They had all heard the chilled steel in the voice of their Queen. "Yes, Your Majesty," they said, in chorus.

CHAPTER 4

"... And this is the Under Chamberlain's Hall, and beyond it are the second-level kitchens. They're only used if the Diplomatic Suite, just above, is occupied. The kitchens were specially set up to cater to the tastes of every kind of visitor, and can prepare dishes from all over the world ..."

Master Longacre's voice went on and on, like the Palace itself. Rhianna had begun to regret asking him for the tour. Perhaps it might have been best to try to explore by herself.

Of course it was fascinating, in a way. Take the hall they were walking through, for example. Master Longacre knew all about it. "... It's over five hundred years old. There was a grand banqueting room just down that way. But that was knocked down after it got damaged in a storm, and the hall was then only used as a short cut. Later it became a gallery to hang King Philemon's pictures in. Some time after that, the pictures were taken down and one half of the hall was turned into offices and storerooms. The other half became this corridor."

Rhianna looked down the dim length of it. "And the doors on *both* sides?" she asked, for doors of different heights and sizes were set at odd intervals along the walls. Some looked as though they hadn't been opened in a very long time. One or two had little steps leading up or down to them.

Master Longacre shrugged. "Well, other buildings were built adjoining it, and doors were put through the walls to connect with them. Some of those buildings were then knocked down, or burned down, or altered. So some windows look out on to little courtyards, others on to blank walls, and others were blocked up altogether."

It was a rabbit's warren, thought Rhianna. And it went on and on and on. "What happened to the pictures?" she asked, at random.

Master Longacre seemed a little embarrassed. "Would you believe it, I really don't know. They weren't very good pictures, they say. King Philemon wasn't . . . er . . . well, he wasn't the greatest artist who ever lived, even if *he* thought he was. Perhaps they were put down into the cellars."

"Cellars?" asked Rhianna. "There's more?"

"Oh, yes," said Master Longacre vaguely. "There's cellars and undercrofts and storerooms under most of the Palace. Several layers deep, in places. I'm afraid I don't know all of them."

Rhianna looked thoughtfully at the interesting little doors, and Master Longacre cleared his throat sharply. "I wouldn't suggest you start looking, though, Miss. Some of the old passages are quite dangerous — even above ground. Long neglected, with uneven flagstones and loose boards, even rotten floors and wonky steps. Old wells and pits that have been covered over. That sort of thing. The cellars would be much worse." He walked on, as if he wished to leave the subject behind.

Rhianna felt the prickle of curiosity. It sounded exciting. But she would be silly to go wandering around in this maze of a place. She was far too sensible to do that. Truly.

Anyway, this passageway wasn't secret. In fact, Rhianna had seen it before. Master Longacre took one more turn. "And here we are," he said.

They were outside the door of the rooms that the Wildwoods had been given. "Thank you, Master Longacre," said Rhianna politely, and the Chamberlain nodded.

"A pleasure, Miss Wildwood. Not often that I find someone interested in the workings of the Palace. Do please call on me if I can answer any questions." He bowed and departed, leaving Rhianna to let herself in.

Her mother was there, on her own. "Where are Father and Eris?" asked Rhianna.

Mrs. Wildwood was mending a stocking. "They went out to look at forges," she answered, biting off the thread. She shook her head. "Some holiday! Not two days away from his shop, and your father's itching to have a hammer in his hands again. And Eris, bless her, is just as bad. They're probably annoying some poor smith right now."

It had been Father and Eris who had driven Rhianna out that morning. They had begun talking over breakfast, and they had gone on and on. Father had been full of details about the sword, about its look, feel, metal, working, and decoration, and Eris had asked questions and nodded. They were using blacksmithing words, too. Rhianna had understood about one in three.

But she was used to that by now. She knew that her father's work was the most important thing in his world to him, after his family. And indeed, Eriseth was sort of family now, anyway. Almost an elder sister.

Rhianna smiled, got out her workbook, and began a sort of a map of the Palace. It wasn't easy. She drew a square for the room she was in and others for the bedrooms and then the corridor outside. Then there was a twisty little staircase *that* way, and a curve that went *this* way . . .

She was still drawing, trying to get the distances and the directions right, when there was a knock on the door. It was Northstar. He had come to take her to the Library of Wizardly College. There were books there on every subject under the sun, not only magic.

"It must be a very large library," remarked Rhianna. She closed the book and stood up, putting it under her arm.

"Mm? Oh, yes. Enormous." Magister Northstar seemed a little distracted. "Fills up two great rooms. The books on magic, which are the main concern of the College, are only the first room."

They walked along an echoing hall — a different one — and descended a staircase that twisted unexpectedly in the middle. The corridor at the bottom ran in a different direction altogether.

A man in wizard's robes passed by going the other way, and they exchanged nods, the other wizard looking a little oddly at Rhianna. A moment later, the Magister turned sharply, pulled open one of a pair of doors in the side of the corridor, and ushered Rhianna through. She walked three steps into the room beyond, and then stopped short. Her mouth opened. Her gaze rose. Suddenly, she felt very small indeed.

It was a room so big that it echoed, and all the walls were made of books. A sweep of shelves ran up to the roof on all sides, far above her head. To reach the higher ones, there were ladders on runners. Every shelf was full of books. Fat brown books, tall thin books, books with green and blue and yellow corners, books with gold edging, great heavy books lying on their sides, books and books and more books. Light streamed down from tall thin windows in between the shelves. The floor was made of polished wood, and on it, crowded in, were more shelves of books. There were more books here than Rhianna had thought were in the whole world.

She looked around, mouth still open, and Magister Northstar leaned on his staff and watched her. Perhaps he was thinking about the first time he had seen this room, many years before, and he smiled a little.

Rhianna's eyes were still on the shelves of books, wonder in her face, when he spoke: "There's a copy here of every book written by any of the Mages of Wizardly College, past and present. Many other books of magic as well. But" — he swept a hand around — "these are all about the High Magic, the magic of Word and Hand, Sign and Rune, that wizards practice. That's not *your* magic, Rhianna."

Rhianna still looked up. Her lips moved. "No," she whispered.

"Your magic is the Wild Magic. It needs no signs or spells. It comes direct from the Land and the Waters to you and through you, fresh and strong — and uncontrolled. We wizards learn the spells that call and shape our power. But you are different. You don't *call* magic — it comes to you without calling. And it comes easily. Too easily, as you have found. You must know perfectly what you are trying to do, and use only enough Wild Magic to do your will, and no more. What's left over is uncontrolled, and terribly dangerous. It isn't called Wild for nothing."

Rhianna nodded, looking down. She remembered the living iron dogs that she had made, and had to unmake, with such pain. She knew what came of not controlling her magic.

"So," continued Northstar, "the books you really need are through here." He turned and walked across the great room. Rhianna followed him.

Set among the shelves was a small, low door with a ring-latch. Magister Northstar twisted and pulled, and the door opened with a creak. He ushered Rhianna through and followed her.

"These are the books that aren't about magic," he said, and looked around him. "This was the Royal Library of King Roger. Not so many people use it, these days," he added, apologetically.

Indeed it did look disused. There was a musty smell in the air, and the light from the tall windows was much dimmed by dirt. There was a fireplace in one corner, but otherwise it was the same as the other — the rooms might have been a pair. They were crammed to the ceiling with shelves, all full of books. But here there were also piles of books on the floor and the two tables, and others leaning against the walls.

Magister Northstar tutted. "I shall have to speak to the Librarian," he said. "We must organize this a little better." He picked up a book that had fallen down, and read the name on its spine. "Hum. *On Light*. Well. Speaking of light, let's have some in."

He pushed on the window, but it wouldn't open, and the pane was thick with dust. "Really!" he exclaimed. He began wiping dust from the windowpane with a white handkerchief. A little more light started to come through, but there was a lot of window that was out of reach.

He looked down at the hankerchief, which was now not as white as it had been. "I had no idea we had let King Roger's Library get like this. Why, this is disgraceful." He put the handkerchief in his pocket and wiped his hands. "I must talk to the Librarian about it. You can't read in here as it is."

Rhianna looked around in the dim light, and silently agreed. The dust tickled her nose. It lay on everything, a fluffy gray coating like dirty frost. On the table just by her, among the tumbled books, it was thick enough to write her name in.

"We could try a sort of banishing spell on the dust," she said. "That would get rid of it."

Northstar shook his head. "We could," he replied. "If we wanted to risk getting rid of some of the books as well. That dust is mostly crumbled paper and powdered ink, you know. Are you sure you could banish the dust, and only the dust, and not the paper and ink that are still in the books? I think I could, but it would take a lot of doing. Cleaning cloths and buckets of water are much easier."

Rhianna nodded. Besides, using magic to do what you could and should do for yourself was a waste of it.

Northstar walked to the door. "I'll go and find the Librarian, Rhianna. Perhaps you can make a start — there's a broom closet in the other room, and I'm sure I've seen a dustpan and brush in there, as well as mops. Just don't climb on the shelves." He stepped through.

Rhianna nodded. She followed him. In the other room, she found the broom closet as Northstar left by the far door in search of the Librarian. His footsteps faded. She fetched in a pan and brush, a broom and a couple of dust cloths, put them on the table by the door, and wondered where she should start.

The light was dim, as Magister Northstar had said — too dim to read by. Rhianna looked around. Perhaps she could start with the windows. She should be able to reach the lower panes if she stood on the sill.

She had to put some big flat books in a pile to climb on before she could reach even that high, but she began to ply her cloth and her brush on the window panes. It was dirty work, and soon the dust was flying. Rhianna sneezed, once, twice, three times. *Once for luck, twice for news, three times for a warning.* That was what her mother said.

Or three times for a lot of dust, thought Rhianna. But now more light was coming through, bright bars of it striking down to the hardwood floor. That floor had been polished once, she saw, but the smooth floorboards had been overlaid with more dust — a lot of dust. There was so much that she could clearly see her footprints in it, now that the light was so much better. There they were, and there were Magister Northstar's, too. And there . . .

There was a third set in the dust on the floor. Rhianna looked down at the tracks. Yes. There they were, a single line of footprints, left foot, right foot, walking across the room from the door, going over to the far wall. Neither Rhianna nor Northstar had gone over there, and so they must belong to someone else. How interesting! At least one other person used this room. Or had used it, at least once. She wondered who it was; perhaps they were interested in the books, too.

Rhianna wished Eriseth were with her. Eris would have read the marks and known all about the person who had made them, man or woman, how old they were, whether they had been carrying anything, if they were in a hurry, how long ago they had been there . . . everything. She had taught Rhianna a little about tracking, and . . . wait a moment. Rhianna looked again. Yes. Yes indeed. Eriseth would need to see this, and as soon as possible. This was really quite odd. For there was only one set of tracks. Their maker had walked up to the wall, and had not walked back. It was as if whoever it was had disappeared into thin air or flown away.

She had turned and begun climbing down when she heard the outer door open and close, and with it, voices. One of them was Magister Northstar's. The little door in the wall of books opened, and Magister Northstar stepped through.

"There, you see," he said as he walked in. "Shelves disordered, books in piles higgledy-piggledy everywhere. It's musty and damp, and the windows were so dirty one needed a candle to read — and on a sunny summer's day, too. My apprentice has done a bit of cleaning already, I see, but it's just a scrape. This really won't do, Master Librarian."

The other was a small man, older than Northstar, and bent. He had long, wispy white hair and a scant beard, and his dark blue robe trailed on the floor. He wrung his hands. "I'm sorry, Magister, but there's only so much I can do. There's only me to look after the whole library, and I've my hands full in the main room. It's not as if the books here are about magic, you know." He waved at the disorder, as if to ask, *What's all the fuss about?*

Magister Northstar drew himself up. "This is the College Library, and it was King Roger's before that. It must be cared for better than this. If you can't manage it yourself, get some apprentices in to help you."

The Librarian's gaze traveled around the room. It stopped when it came to Rhianna, who was still standing on the windowsill, trying to look as small as possible. His eyebrows lifted. "Apprentices?" he said. "If we are to use apprentices, Magister, what about starting with yours? It seems as though she'll be the major customer, here."

Northstar frowned. "Rhianna has already done some work. And she needs to study. You know how important her Wild Magic is."

"Oh, everyone knows how *special* she is, Magister. But surely she can study and tidy up a bit as she goes. After all, it would be a wonderful way to get to know the library." The Librarian was smiling, but the smile did not reach his eyes.

Northstar and Rhianna exchanged glances. For her part, Rhianna was surprised at how little the Librarian seemed to like the idea of somebody having the Wild Magic.

Northstar looked cross. For a moment, it seemed as if he would refuse. But he nodded. "Very well," he said. "Rhianna, it wouldn't hurt to do some dusting and reshelving. You can start right away — I see that you've already done quite a bit." He turned. "But see here, Librarian, my apprentice is not a cleaner. She is here to learn. See you get some others in here to help. I want to see order and light restored before the week is out."

The Librarian bowed, though Rhianna thought it was not with goodwill. "Yes, Magister," he replied, and at the same time shot a look at her. "By your leave, I'll be about it right away." He bowed again and stepped through the door, which closed behind him.

Northstar shook his head. Rhianna climbed down from the sill. "He doesn't seem happy," she said.

"No, he does not. Always was a stick-in-the-mud, but now . . ." He shook his head once more, hesitated a moment, then spoke again. "Rhianna, I've been doing a little quiet listening and talking to a few of the wizards, the people I trust. It seems that Odderer was right, and I may owe him an apology. There's a lot of talk about you and your Wild Magic, and it's clear that some people resent you. You're the first Wild Talent in, oh, ever so many years. They fear — and they're right to fear — a Wild Talent that might go wrong. They don't know you as I do. So we must bear with them for a while, until they do."

Rhianna nodded. She understood. And she knew that it would never do to make trouble for her master. He looked worried, too, probably about his magical sword, and she could see she had no right to add to his worries. Still, the sooner Eriseth saw the marks in the dust the better.

"Yes, Magister," she said.

CHAPTER 5

"You should see it, Eris! The tracks go right up to the wall and stop. You should come soon, before they clear it all away."

"Tomorrow," said Eriseth of Arwensgrove. She ate a piece of apple. Supper was laid out in the sitting room, and a Palace steward stood by the wall to serve them. Mr. and Mrs. Wildwood ate without speaking. Eris used her clasp-knife to cut another slice of apple. "I'll come and see it tomorrow. It sounds interesting. But you haven't asked us what *we've* been doing today."

Rhianna blinked. She had been so taken up with her own day as to leave out the doings of others. Now that she looked, she could see a sort of shared excitement between her father and Eriseth, a we've-got-a-secret smile. "What is it?" asked Rhianna, and, when they still smiled that same smile, "Come on, tell me!"

Mr. Wildwood picked up his own knife and plucked a

ripe peach out of the bowl. He began to peel it. "We went to see some people I know. There was Griff Tummis, who was apprentice with me in old Widgery's works, before we came out to Smallhaven. And Nat Buckle, and a few others. Good craftsmen, all of them." He cut a slice off the peach and ate it.

Rhianna made *go on* noises. Her father glanced at Eriseth, and she took it up. "We were trying to find out something about that sword."

"But Father just said his friends were good craftsmen, and that no good smith would ever make such a thing."

Eriseth nodded. "Yes, but a good smith knows who the bad ones are. Word gets around. Every smith builds up a list of places that he'd never send sparc customers to, no matter how busy his own shop might be. So we asked about bad smiths, and we asked about striking patterns."

"Striking patterns?" asked Rhianna.

"Yes," said Mr. Wildwood, pushing his chair back. "Ah. That's better. Did a lot of walking today. Avalon's a lot bigger than I remember." The servant began to clear the plates. "Thank you. Yes, striking patterns. Every smith uses a hammer a little differently, because every smith has different hands and shoulders and arms. We make our own tools to suit ourselves, too. So it's not surprising that each smith's striking pattern, the way they use a hammer, is as different as their handwriting — if they could all write. I remember that sword, and I'm sure I'd recognize that pattern if I ever saw it again."

Rhianna felt a pang of disappointment. "But you haven't," she said.

"I haven't *yet*." Mr. Wildwood grimaced. "I found one or two bad smiths, though. From now on I"ll have to act like a customer. Somebody looking for a cheap repair job. I can spare Eriseth for a while. Go and look at your tracks, and I'll tell you what I've found out, tomorrow."

The sun was up early, but it was only just above the hills behind the city when Rhianna opened the door and showed Eriseth into King Roger's Library. Eriseth looked up at the shelves of books, disbelief in her face.

"And these are all full of writing?" she asked in a whisper. Rhianna nodded. "And all of the writings are different?" Rhianna nodded again. "*Coedwig hen*, there can't be anything left in the world to write!"

It was as it had been. They stood there looking at the dust and the books. Rhianna had cleaned the windows as high as she could reach, and clear morning light streamed through. The rest of the room was untouched — she knew enough not to tread on a trail. After a swift, disbelieving stare around the shelves, Eriseth shook her head and turned her attention to the prints in the dust.

"A man," said Eris, after a brief glance, "and quite tall. See the length of his stride, and how he was wearing a broad heel, and turned his feet out? His shoes were a little worn, but good cobbling, made for him. He was wearing a long gown, for it brushed on the foot of that table leg there. Difficult to say when he passed — I don't know how fast the dust falls in here. A week ago, perhaps. And yes, you're right. He walked straight up to that wall, stood there a moment, and then stepped through."

Rhianna stared at her. "Stepped through?" she asked. "What, straight through the wall?" She looked across the room at the shelves, rank on rank, where the tracks stopped.

"No," said Eriscth. "Through a door. It opens away, or there'd be a mark. But there's a door there." She padded over to the wall, following the trail of prints, stepping almost in them, while Rhianna stayed where she was, not to confuse the trail. Eriseth inspected the rows of books. "Yes, here."

She pulled a book out from the shelves. "Here. The dust has been disturbed. That was at about the same time as the prints were made, too. And here . . ." she pointed at a small pile of ashes on the shelf, behind the book. "Here he burned something. There's a scorch mark. Can't have been much, though. A little scrap of paper. There's a drop of wax there, too. He was carrying a candle, and used it to light the paper. But what I can't see . . . is the door itself. The wall behind the books is smooth plaster over stone. Hear it." She knocked on it. There was nothing but the solid *tunk!* of hard wall.

"The door is hidden, then," said Rhianna, and she felt her pulse increase. A secret passage. And someone who used it. She followed in the footsteps, but when she came within a stride of the wall, a prickle of tiny sharp claws walked up her back. She stopped short.

"More than hidden," Eris was saying, her back to Rhianna. "I've got eyes. There's no crack, no join, and no line to hide it. The plaster is smooth and white and the shelves are unbroken. I know there's a door there because I know, just as if I'd seen him do it, that a man stepped through it. What I just can't see is how . . . What's the matter?"

"There's magic there." Rhianna felt she should be whispering. "Old magic. Quiet, like a wave that only gathers its powers when it reaches the shore, but just as strong."

"Oh?" Eriseth stared at the wall again. "Well, that would explain it. I can't see anything, but it must be here. Come, help me look." Her voice was calm and certain.

Rhianna shook herself. She stared at the wall, at the shelves that Eriseth had said must open, but there was no crack or join. Yet the magic was clear as a signpost. She passed a hand over the wall, and it was there. Then she looked down at the tiny pile of gray ash on the shelf, and her skin prickled anew.

"They're connected, somehow," she whispered. "Eris, the paper he burned and the magic of the door are connected. It's like they were . . . two halves of the same spell."

She stared at the little pile of ashes, and thought. There was a rule in magic. *Anything unmade can be remade. Things once joined can be joined again.* She thought of the paper that it had been, those ashes.

Oh, it was a small enough task. A tiny pinch of the Wild Magic would do it, but it must be controlled, hedged about. She took a deep breath and slipped the necklace off, putting it on the shelf before her.

As always, magic flowed in from the world around her. The sun of high summer streaming in at the window, the cold deep bones of the castle and the earth beneath, the running sea in the harbor, the warm breeze, all brought the Wild Magic to her. It filled her, easily, quickly, and she had to fight it for a moment. But she held it, and she looked at the ashes, and saw them as they were, and as they had been. Rhianna gave a tiny release of power, like a careful breath.

Eriseth gasped. This was always a wonder to her, this

magic that Rhianna could make at will, without word or sign or spell. The ashes stirred on the shelf. They twitched into a new pattern, laying themselves out flat in a square three fingers wide. The gray surface became white, then yellowish, the color of old bone. Out of the air, dark particles fell like tiny raindrops, and they made a pattern on the square. They came together in loops and swirls that became letters. There it was, a small square of old parchment with writing on it.

"It's a message," breathed Eriseth. Rhianna blinked, and held the Wild Magic in. She picked up her necklace, and instantly the magic in her blew out like a candle. As always, she had to ignore the feeling that she had made herself blind and dumb, and that the world was somehow made less.

She shook herself, and stared at the scrap of paper she had remade. "No," she said. "It's a rhyme." She read it through, slowly:

A hollow voice calls from the trees,
Pass pathless bridge, turn lockless keys,
Bend arrowless bow, scratch crying cat,
And I'll sing sweet if you do that.

Eriseth nodded, as if it made sense. "It's a riddle," she said. "Just like the ones the Eldra tell around their fires in the forest. You have to say what it is."

"And it's a half of the spell. So it's a password, too."

"Well, we can find it. I am Eldra, and we know how to answer riddles. What is hollow that comes from trees?"

Rhianna scratched her head. "Walnut shells?" she asked.

Eriseth looked dubious. "I don't think so. It has to have a voice. I was thinking *the wind in the leaves*, but I don't see where a roadless bridge or a key that doesn't have a lock comes in. Or cats, either. And what good's a bow without arrows?"

"It might be one that's not meant to shoot arrows. Just as it could mean a bridge that isn't for carrying a road, or a key that isn't made to open locks. Things that are just called that, bow or keys or bridge. Hollow from the trees, though . . . a boat! That's hollow, and it comes from trees — it's made of wood."

"No. But you've got something there. Something wooden and hollow. And something that has keys, and a bridge, and a bow, and a sweet voice, and . . ."

It was as if both were touched with a hand on both their shoulders at the same moment. Both called out loud: "A violin!"

For a moment, there was a deep stillness in the room, like a dog wondering if it really had to obey or not. Then there was a creak, and a line appeared in the wall. The shelf of books before them and the wall itself rose smoothly from the floor, straight up into the ceiling, disappearing into a sort of upside-down well in the roof. It rose until a narrow doorway the height of a tall man was revealed. It was the top of a staircase, and the steps curved away into the darkness, downwards and out of sight.

CHAPTER 6

The Eldra could both see and hear better than the people they called the Clumsy Ones. People like Rhianna. Eriseth stared down into the darkness. Then she shook her head. There was a damp breath out of the opening, cool against the summer breeze. She wrinkled her nose.

"It goes a long way. I can hear the sea, and smell it, but nothing else. There's nobody there now. Whoever it was, he isn't just out of sight, waiting for us. But I'm still not going down there without a light and the proper gear."

Rhianna nodded. However much she wanted to go exploring, she knew sense when she heard it. Anyway, her master should know of this. "We won't try now. I'll tell Magister Northstar. And I've a feeling we shouldn't tell anyone else, not until he says it's all right. This is someone who used a secret, magic-locked passageway in the castle, and who didn't want to be followed."

Eriseth peered into the dark space again, then flicked a glance up at the door. "How do we close it?" she asked.

"Step back, and I'll try the same word."

It worked. Rhianna said *"Violin,"* and the door slid smoothly down into place. The crack around the edge blended into the plaster and disappeared, and a moment later anyone would swear that there was no possibility of a door being there. They were left staring at the place it had been.

"Well," Rhianna said. "Perhaps I should start dusting in here. Magister Northstar said he'd look in sometime today. I'll tell him about it then."

Eriseth glanced out of the tall, narrow windows. The sun was still only just over the horizon. "All right," she said. "I'll go and get some things — rope, chalk, a couple of lights . . . and my bow. You come up to the rooms when you've seen your master. I can spend today on this — tomorrow I'll be helping mine."

She slipped out. Rhianna knew she would find her way back all right — Eriseth never lost it. And now for the cleaning. Being the apprentice to a wizard, even the greatest wizard in Avalon, wasn't all fun. She picked up a broom and a dust cloth, and began.

About mid-morning another apprentice arrived, a pimply lad a year or two older than Rhianna. He said nothing at all, sniffed at the state the library was in, and dawdled about, flicking a rag at some of the worst of the dust. At noon he disappeared, and did not return. Rhianna worked grimly on. A little along the corridor outside, she found a door that opened into a small courtyard where there was a fountain. That gave her water to mop with. As the summer sun reached its height and started its long descent the library grew warm, and Rhianna had to wipe her brow as she worked, clearing books and reshelving them, wiping down the tables, using a ladder from the room next door to reach higher on the windows.

She was easing her back when the door rattled and opened. Magister Northstar walked in. "Ah," he said. "That's better."

The tables were clear and dusted, the floor was swept, and clear light streamed down. It was still musty, for Rhianna had not been able to open the windows, but the disorder and dirt and piles of books were cleared away. He nodded.

"You've done enough cleaning for today, Rhianna. And a good job you've made of it, too. . . . What is it? You're jumping about like a hen with an egg and no nest."

"Magister . . . there's something that you must see . . ."

A minute later, Northstar was staring down into the

hidden stairwell himself, and listening as Rhianna told how she had found it. He picked up the scrap of paper with the riddle on it and stroked his beard.

"And only Eriseth knows of this?" he asked. Rhianna nodded. "Good. She can keep a closed mouth, that one. And a closed mouth is needed, for the time being. There's something going on in the College that I don't care for." He rubbed thumb and finger gently over the paper and stared into the dark space. "I've never heard of this. I should have been told by whoever found it, but I was not. And more, it's clear that someone has been spreading tales about you. One of the College wizards actually asked if it wasn't a little dangerous, allowing you to make *monsters*. Monsters, if you please! She'd heard some stupid story or other. I put her right, but there's malice there, and I don't like it. And now this." He shook his head. "It's got so I'm not sure who to trust."

Rhianna looked up into his eyes, and they were dark with worry. "You can trust me, master," she said gently. "You said so, and it's true."

He smiled at her. "So I did, and so it is. And I can trust Eriseth and your parents, too." He eyed the dark stairwell, considering a moment. "Very well. I need to know what this is, and I also need to find out what's going on in the College. I am best to work on the College, and you and Eriseth are best to explore. I think that between your

Wild Magic and her Eldra knowledge, you will find what there is to find. You may follow this up, but carefully, carefully, Rhianna. Take Eriseth with you."

Rhianna pushed down a bubble of excitement. This was just what she had hoped for. "Yes, Magister," she said. "I will do as you say."

Her master smiled, but it was a strained smile. "I think you will, since it's what you want to do. In fact, I think I'd have trouble stopping you. I have enough sense not to swim against a torrent, and that's what your Wild Magic is. Indeed, it's a torrent that you must learn to measure against the world, and soon. So I must let you try now." He looked away again, at the opening in the wall and the staircase. "But I don't like this."

"Come on, Eris, let's go!"

Eriseth looked up from the table. She raised one eyebrow as Rhianna hopped from one foot to the other, and she continued to put things into her leather pack, working slowly and carefully. Lanterns, spare oil, flint and steel for striking a light, thin strong rope of Eldra make, bread, cheese, a bottle of water, a piece of chalk, thread, spare bowstrings, an oilskin. Already she was wearing her small, sharp knife in its sheath on her belt, with her quiver and her arrows. Her bow stood by the door, the Eldra longbow that Rhianna couldn't even bend, let alone pull the string to her ear, as Eriseth could. Eris was a lot stronger than she looked.

At last she nodded, and they returned to King Roger's library. Again it was quiet and empty — clearly, the Librarian had made no great effort to find others to help clean it. They stood before the wall, and again Rhianna said the password, and again there was a pause before the door showed itself and slid smoothly upwards.

The stairs were as before. Eriseth was striking a light, as sure here as she was in the forest, and in a moment she had the lanterns lit. She handed one to Rhianna.

"Now," she said, and her voice meant *no nonsense, Rhianna.* "We go single file, me first. You step where I step. When I wave like this, you stop. Make as little noise as you can."

That meant, of course, that Eriseth would be making no noise at all.

Rhianna nodded. She would do her best, but she knew she would never match Eris for that. They stepped into the opening and Rhianna closed the door behind them.

They stood now at the top of a set of old stone steps that led down and curved gently to the right between solid stone walls. Eriseth started down, testing each tread before trusting it. In a dozen steps they were out of sight of the door, and in two dozen they had come to the bottom of the staircase.

They found themselves in a space, damp and smelling slightly of the sea. Eriseth raised her lantern, and the wan light played over a stone floor stretching out into the gloom. The floor was uneven, made of worn stone slabs. The wall ran left and right behind them to corners, ten paces off. The ceiling seemed to be natural rough stone, too.

Rhianna stared around, and suddenly she gasped. There were eyes looking at her out of the gloom on both sides, narrow eyes, calculating. She stepped backwards, a sudden coldness at her spine. Eriseth hissed. Her hand flashed to her arrows, and she might have been about to drop the lantern.

But the movement made no change in the shadows, and the eyes stayed fixed, staring. A moment later, Rhianna and Eriseth saw what it was — painted figures on each of the side walls, a file of marching men done in earthy colors, red-browns and black and white, all striding stiffly together away into the darkness. The whites of their eyes stood out. The paint was cracked and flaking, and pieces of the plaster had fallen away, but you could still see the picture. What were they marching towards?

Eriseth padded away into the gloom, and Rhianna followed. A moment later, the Eldra girl stopped short, holding up a hand. Then she moved on again, the lantern light around her like a bubble. The wall on the other side of the room loomed up. On it, the soldiers had turned inwards, and marched towards a stone platform, one step high, that was set against the far wall. In that wall was another doorway.

"A doorway, but no door," Eriseth murmured. Through it was another room. They listened. Perhaps the waves of the sea could be heard through the stone, a slow tolling like some huge far-off drum, but nothing more. Eriseth jerked her head and stepped into the opening.

It was the same as before, but smaller. Little chips of stone lay scattered on the bare floor, but otherwise the room was bare and empty. Again, the walls were painted, this time with pictures of people at a banquet, the table running around the wall with the diners sitting stiffly behind it. Two more doorways led off to left and right.

"Wait," said Rhianna, fumbling her book out of her pack. "I'll start making a map." Eriseth said nothing as she drew. Then they moved on again. Eris, shrugging, took the left-hand opening, marking it as she did.

It took them some time — Rhianna wasn't sure how long. There was no way of telling the time, unless they counted their heartbeats. But after a while, it began to make sense. This had been a suite of connecting rooms. There were five of them. There were no doors, though you could see where there had been hinges for them once. And in only one room was there any sort of furniture.

This was a sunken oval in the middle of the floor, three finger-widths deep. It was just the right size to sit in with your knees drawn up. In the bottom, small flat stones had been cemented down. Around the rim other stones stuck up unevenly, forming a ragged edge around it.

"What's that?" asked Eriseth. Rhianna looked, and the shape of the hole reminded her of something. A moment later, she had worked out what it was.

"It's a bath," she exclaimed. "Just the bottom of one. The rest has been broken up and taken away."

Eriseth nodded and looked around. "So this was a bathroom," she said.

But Rhianna was frowning. Something wasn't quite right. She looked at her map again. This bathroom — if it was a bathroom — was in between two larger, square rooms. "I suppose those were bedrooms, then," she said, mostly to herself. "But who'd want to live in a hole like a mole?"

Eriseth had heard her — Eriseth heard most things. "I think it wasn't a hole, once." She nodded at a square of roughly laid unplastered brick in the wall. "I think that was a window, but it's been blocked up. Badly. Some of the bricks are coming loose." She looked about in the gloom. "I think that these rooms were here before they started building the Palace, only they were above ground then. They wanted the castle to stand as high as possible on the headland, so they built up the foundations, and these old stone buildings on the site were covered over and turned into cellars. Then the castle and the Palace got rebuilt and changed so many times that the cellars got built over, again and again — and eventually forgotten."

"But who made the secret door? Whoever it was went to a lot of trouble to hide it."

"Perhaps you should ask King Roger. It was in his library, after all."

Rhianna shook her head. The paintings on the walls of this room showed a net full of fish and other sea creatures, and a fisherman on one side pulling them in to shore. The water was shown with wavy brown lines, and the fisherman at work was as stiffly drawn as the diners at the formal banquet. But yes. Plainly, the square in the wall had been an opening once.

There was a short silence. Not quite silence. Again they heard the low rumble of the waves beating on the headland. Rhianna looked at the fisherman and the waves painted on the damp walls, and something jogged in her head. "Water," she said. Eriseth glanced at her, eyebrows raised. Rhianna waved a hand at the broken bath. "This was a bathroom. Where did the water for it come from?"

Eriseth nodded in appreciation. "Good question. A spring, perhaps? Maybe a well?"

"A well, I think. We'd hear a spring. But where was it?"

"We can hear a well, too. Or I could, if you'll stand as still as possible and try not to breathe too loudly."

Now, that was new, even to Rhianna, who knew more than most people of what Eriseth could do. But she nodded, and stood as still as a stone while the Eldra hunter tapped her bowstave on the ground and turned her head from side to side, questing for an echo that only she could hear — and finding it. Step by step, with advances and retreats, she followed it out of the door and into the passage from the banquet room. There she stopped short, then rapped on one side wall, then the other.

"Here," she said. "It's hollow."

She had tapped a piece of paneled stone wall, no different from the others to look at. But indeed it rang hollow. Rhianna looked at it carefully. "This one isn't disguised by magic," she said. "It's just difficult to see."

"Yes," said Eriseth, inspecting the panel. "And it opens outwards. See the scuff marks on the floor there? The crack is hidden by that paint-line, but I should have noticed before. Now, where's the latch? There must be one. Someone had to draw water from here. Ah!"

One of the edges of the panel was slightly raised, just enough so that it was possible to slide a finger underneath. A tug, and the stone panel opened towards them like a cupboard door. It was low and narrow. Within were three steps down into a little domed round chamber. In the middle of the chamber was a low wall, also circular.

Eriseth raised her lantern and they moved down the steps the same way as before. The dampness in the air increased. This would have been below even the old ground level. At the wall, Rhianna leaned over and looked down into blackness. Far below, she thought to see the light of her lamp reflecting off water.

"It's a well, all right," she said, turning to Eriseth.

But Eriseth was looking at the far side of the chamber. She squinted in the shadows, and then hissed between her teeth. "That's not all it is. See there?"

There was another opening in the wall. It was irregular and broken, just big enough for one person to squeeze through, and bits of stone lay on the floor around it. "And there," added Eriseth, pointing.

She was pointing at an old wooden bucket lying on the floor. It had a rope handle, and another rope for pulling it up lay coiled on the floor beside it. Eriseth stared, then padded over to it, squatted down and felt the rope.

She looked up, rocked back on her heels, and nodded, as if confirming something. "The rope's wet," she said. "Someone used it not long ago. Today or yesterday, no more." She stared around at the little room. It was musty. Here the walls were not plastered, but made of slabs of stone. "Someone needed to draw water. Why?"

Rhianna had gone to the entrance to the narrow passage, and moved a few steps down it. Then she stopped. "I think I can tell you why," she said.

CHAPTER 7

"It was a bundle of clothes. Well, rags, really. Scraps of this and that. Old blankets, worn-out cloaks. It looked like a rat's nest, but it was someone's bed. There was a stump of a candle by it, and sooty marks on the wall where it had burned." Rhianna watched the face of her master, and saw concern and dawning realization. "And there were crumbs of food — bread, vegetable peelings. Table scraps, I suppose." She took a deep breath. "Somebody lives down there, Magister."

Eriseth leaned on her bow and said nothing, looking around at the Magister's study, which she had not seen before. Rhianna waited while Northstar stroked his beard. He seemed to spend a long time just thinking.

"Well," he said at last. "Now the kitchen goblin is explained."

"The kitchen goblin, Magister?"

"Yes. It's a story that I hear from time to time from the Head Steward. Food goes missing from the College kitchens every now and then. Not very much. Not enough to set up a market stall or anything. A bag of apples here, bacon there, milk and fruit, a loaf, eggs. The servants talk about the kitchen goblin and make jokes. For a long time the College has just put it down to somebody stealing food, although no one has ever been caught. So we just sighed, and thought that if they needed the food, it was good that they should have it. But now . . ." He trailed off.

"What about now, Magister?"

"Mmm? Well, the point is that I first heard that story when I came to the College as the apprentice of old Master Furoval." He paused. "And that was forty years ago."

Rhianna blinked. Forty years? Someone had been living in the damp dark of the old passages under the Palace for forty years? Her mouth opened and closed, and she stood shocked and amazed. And then a great gush of pity welled up. Poor soul! Forty years in the dark! What had she called it? *Like a mole in a hole.* What on earth could have driven a person to such a life?

Something else occurred to her. "Magister . . . if he can get into the kitchens, there must be other entrances into the Palace from down there. And, come to think of it, the footprints we found led only one way — into the secret entrance, not away from it. So whoever it is walked out of some other entrance and into that one."

Northstar watched her, stroked his beard, and said nothing. Rhianna glanced at Eriseth, but Eris was shaking her head. "The footprints were of a tall man wearing good soft shoes that were made for him not too long ago, and a long robe. Not one who'd been living alone in the dark for a lifetime. Someone else knows of that entrance." She paused. "And that means they probably know of whoever's living under the Palace, too."

Northstar stroked his beard again. "And they didn't tell anyone about it." His voice was distant. Then he nodded. "Very well. I must admit, I like this not at all. Nevertheless, we proceed as before. You are the best to investigate these spaces and passages under the Palace. I will continue asking discreet questions in the College — who's been spending time in King Roger's library, has anyone been asking questions of the kitchen staff, and so on. I am more likely than you to get answers."

Eriseth looked doubtfully at Rhianna. "I must assist my own master in searching for this cheat of a smith, Magister," she said.

"Indeed. So you must, and so you should, for I've a feeling — it's only a feeling — that Rhianna and I hold both ends of the same piece of string. And Master Wildwood holds another, if that is possible. What will we find, I wonder, when we work our way to the tangle in the middle? Go carefully, both of you."

They looked at each other and nodded.

Rhianna's skill at drawing maps was improving. In a week, she had covered half a dozen pages with careful plans of rooms and passages and staircases, both of the Palace itself and the dark spaces below. In the Palace, she was able to place things in relation to one another — "This is the west wall of the Small Lecture Room. On the other side of this wall is the Preparation Room, and over there is the equipment store, so *that* must be . . ."

Things were more difficult in the secret places that she was beginning to call the Underdark. From the well room a narrow passage ran sloping deeper into the earth, three paces long. Then there was a chamber, a room just big enough to lie down in, and here Rhianna had found the bedding. She didn't touch it.

That room opened into a dark, larger space. Rhianna thought it might have been a cellar once. Burn marks were on the walls and ashes still lay in the corners. The roof looked newer than the rest, heavy timber beams supported by stone columns.

Here were more scraps and signs that someone lived here. A wooden bowl and a lamp — just a flat covered jug for oil, with a spout for a wick. Fish bones. Perhaps there was a way down to the sea. Rhianna looked at the bits and pieces, and shook her head. Then she put down her pack and began getting things out of it.

She had been cautious at first. The first few times in the Underdark she had moved stealthily, and she had started at shadows. But it was always only the flickering light of her lamp, and as she explored further, she began to be aware of how dreary life in the Underdark must be. There was something else, too. Everywhere she went in the dusty spaces, there was the feeling of old, cold fear. It was not her fear. No. Something was afraid of her. She could not be afraid of something that was so frightened of her, only sorry, and she had to try to make the fear less terrible.

"I'll just leave these, shall I?" she said aloud. "Look, bread and some cheese and a flask of oil for your lamp. It must be hard to come by down here. And some apples, and my mum's own pickles." She shook out the bundle under her arm. "And here's a warm blanket. You must get cold. I mean you no harm, and I won't bother you. Thank you for letting me look around."

She paced off distances and guessed at directions, and drew her map. There was another opening in the wall, apparently broken through with a hammer, and when she had finished, she moved through it into the next space. Here a set of steps led up to the ceiling, and there was a trapdoor, and noise from the room above. She stood still and listened.

The noise was the clatter of pots, the sound of a scrubbing brush, and water splashing. And bits of conversation: ". . . And so I said to him, well, lah-de-dah, I said, just because you serve at the Masters' table don't get you no favors here. . . . What, *more* pudding basins? How many puddings did they make for those students, anyway . . . ?"

That must be the scullery for the Apprentices' Dining Hall, above. Rhianna paged back in her book and looked at the maps she had already drawn. That was *there*, and she had marked a little trapdoor *there*, behind two washtubs, apparently nailed shut. She had wondered then where it led. Nowhere, it seemed. The Palace was full of doors like that. Rhianna made notes in her book, then retraced her steps. The things that she had left were gone.

It was a week before she had a glimpse. She came every day, spending an hour slowly exploring the Underdark. It wasn't all underground, she found. The rooms were old cellars and storerooms mostly, and some were still in use. Entrances to the ones that were still used were always narrow, with peepholes and listening places, and they were carefully hidden with loose stones or boarded up. But there was always a way through — nails that could be replaced in their holes, stones that pulled out, furniture or shelving in front that could be pushed out of the way. Once, there was a crawlspace that led through a hollow stack of old wine barrels. Rhianna drew maps in her book showing the ways through. She brought a present every day — food, lights, a hank of cord, a penknife. She left them in the same place each time, and each time they were gone when she came back. But she saw and heard no one.

She couldn't spend all her time down there, of course. She was studying, and taking care of the library. She managed to open the windows, and she lit a fire in the grate to dry the air. The damp was no good for the books. And while she was doing that, she found a whole shelf of old storybooks, written in colored inks on stiff crackling paper, with glowing pictures of knights and ladies and dragons. They were wonderful books, beautiful in themselves, with stories of quests and adventures and magic. Rhianna began to read them for her own pleasure, but that gave her an idea . . .

The next day, she sat at the bottom of the steps in the quiet dark of the room under the College scullery, set her lamp to shine on the pages, and opened the old book. "I thought you might like to hear a story," she said loudly. Only silence answered her, but she smiled and began: "Once upon a time . . ."

The shadows seemed to draw in like listeners as she

read aloud. It was a story that was as colorful and quaint as the book itself, and as she read it she let her voice grow soft, and she listened to the silence in the darkness around. Turning a page, she thought she saw a movement out of the corner of her eye, but she ignored it and read on. The tale wove its events together like a bright embroidered pattern, and she followed it, losing herself in the old words, letting her voice carry her out of the closed, chill darkness and up into the sunshine and the free air.

At last, she came to the end. "And so they lived happily ever after," said Rhianna, and sighed, and gently closed the book. As gently, she turned her head, and there he was.

At first she thought of Magister Northstar, because this man also had long white hair and beard. But no. Her master was a small man with a round tummy, and he was always brushed and clean. This was a long skinny scarecrow, dressed in rags, and his hair and beard were a wild tangle, matted with dirt. He sat on the grimy floor across the room from her, his thin shanks pulled up to his ears, and she could see his eyes staring at her. For a moment, they watched each other, curiosity on both their faces. Then Rhianna saw the sudden spurt of fear in those eyes. There was a movement, a patter of feet, and he was gone into the darkness. She sat on, not moving, not trying to see where he'd gone.

"I'll call in again tomorrow. We're having peach cobbler tonight. I'll save some for you, and there's another story here that I think you'll like." She spoke in an ordinary, natural sort of voice, and again only the silence answered her. Yet she sat a while longer, and then got up quietly and left, knowing that he was watching her from some peephole or other.

Three days passed. Rhianna was showing her maps to her master in his study. Eriseth watched and listened, silently.

"There's a peephole just there," she said, pointing. "He can make sure nobody is about in the kitchen, then nip up through *that* trapdoor, raid the pantry, and be back in the dark again in a moment. So there's your kitchen goblin."

Northstar nodded. "Have you seen any more of him, yourself?" he asked.

"Yes," said Rhianna. "He likes the stories I read. He's slowly getting friendlier — well, at least he seems to be less afraid of me. But he never lets me get closer than ten paces or so, and I'm not going to chase him, poor old man." She paused. "I think he's frightened, Magister. Not just of me. Frightened all the time."

Rhianna and Eriseth exchanged glances. The Eldra hunter shuddered. "It must be a horrible life he leads," she remarked.

The Magister shook his head. "Horrible is right. But I give you my word, we shall have him out of there and looked after, if he will allow it. I think that reading stories to him is just the right thing to do. Be careful not to frighten him further, and when this business is finished with, we'll see what can be done." He looked up and out of the window of his study, which had a view of the busy harbor and the ships in the bright sunlight. Seabirds flew on the warm breeze. He shook his head again. "And has there been any sign of anybody else down there?" he asked.

Rhianna looked down at her maps again. "I'm . . . not sure. I found a little bag of barley sugars a few days ago, and it was new — paper not damp, but crisp and shiny — a bag from a sweet shop. I suppose he might have found it in the kitchens. He likes sweets. That was why I thought he'd like stories."

"Hmm. And Eriseth, what of you and Master Wildwood, and your search for the maker of that sword?"

Eriseth frowned. "I think we're getting closer. My master says he's certain now that it's not any of the regular smiths, not even the cheap ones. He found a couple of pieces — just repairs, both of them, and badly done — that might have the same marks on them. Only it's difficult to be sure, because they were made with different sets of hammers." She paused and looked up at them expectantly, as if she thought that should mean something to them.

They just watched her, puzzlement on their faces, and she sighed. "That means that the work was done by someone who didn't have his own tools to use. He was borrowing or, more likely, hiring them. Not a journeyman or a regular apprentice even. Makes it harder to find him. It might be that nobody knows him at all."

"But someone hired their forge and tools to him, you think. There can't be too many smiths who'd do that."

"No, there aren't. Certainly none of the busy ones. Probably a workshop that isn't doing so well, and of course they'd rather not admit to it." She shrugged. "My master is going around the cheap places looking for someone who'll hire out." She paused. "He hates doing it."

Rhianna grimaced. She could imagine how her father felt about it. Shoddy work was something that he found hard to bear, in smithing above all else — it was dead against everything he was. She went to bed that night with the feeling that something had to happen soon, or he'd start to fret.

She needn't have worried. Three days later, something did.

CHAPTER 8

The day started well. Rhianna had spent a good deal of the previous one on her hands and knees, finding her way down a long low tunnel that ran from the cellars all the way down to the sea at the bottom of the headland. It ended in a pool that swirled and surged in time to the boom of the waves outside. Salt tidemarks were on the rough stone walls. When she covered her lantern, she could see daylight in the water. It must connect with the sea outside.

But it had been tiring work, and she had had no time for reading. In fact, she hadn't seen the old man at all. She had gone to bed early, before her father had returned from the city. He had been very late. But here he was, over breakfast, looking pleased.

"I think I've found our man," he said, buttering toast. "Or nearly. There was a workshop, of sorts" — he grimaced — "and the smith tried to make out that he didn't know what I was talking about. But I saw the look on the face of his apprentice, and I was waiting when they finished for the day. The boss slunk off early, of course, leaving the apprentice to finish up. So I stood him a drink or three, and soon we were talking like old chums."

"So now you know who made the sword, Father?" Rhianna felt her pulse quicken.

But Mr. Wildwood shook his head. "Not by name. I got a good description, though. He's a jobber they see sometimes. What's more, the apprentice remembers a second sword. A rush job, he said, and he was paid to pump the bellows only three days ago. The point is, now I know where I can find that jobber. He hawks scrap iron around the trade and does the odd repair when he's sober, which is not often, apparently. But there's a tavern he's fond of, and lately he's had money. A bad sign, that."

Mrs. Wildwood looked disapproving. "Loys, I'm not sure I like the idea of you spending time in low taverns. Even less when you talk about it in front of Rhianna. Why not hand what you know over to Magister Northstar — or to that Captain of the Guard, what was his name . . . ?"

"Lysandus. But he's on leave still, and I don't think he was very pleased with being told to look in Avalon, anyway. As for Magister Northstar, I want to make sure I actually have what he needs before I bother him. He's got rather a lot of worries, just at the moment." He looked across at his wife. "I'll know by tonight. Then we can tell him. Remember, once we find whoever made that cheat, we can find the person who bespelled it. And when we find him — or her — we can go home. The sooner, the better."

With that, Mrs. Wildwood had to be content. She sipped her tea and said nothing more.

Rhianna prepared for the day. She spent an hour or two in the library, where she was studying as Magister Northstar had recommended, and then she took one of the old storybooks down into the Underdark.

She hurried through the painted rooms, not noticing their walls now, and then into the others, the cellars and spaces that had been connected with little openings and passageways. In the room under the scullery, she sat on the bottom step and took out the book. She opened it and held it up so that the lamplight played on the colored pages.

"Isn't that beautiful?" she asked.

By now she knew that he was looking forward to her visits, though this was the first in three days. He was there, too, sitting in his usual place when she looked up. But this time something was different. He was sitting in an odd position, his right leg twisted and pushed out in front of him. She squinted in the gloom, and a moment later had seen what was wrong. There was blood on his leg, and something was wrong with the ankle.

"You're hurt!" she exclaimed. "Oh, please! Let me help, please let me. That looks nasty. It needs cleaning, and a bandage. Please."

He shied and shook his head, and made as if to stand, but the leg failed him. Perhaps it was that, or something about her voice, or the instant concern on her face, but then he sat still again. He shivered, but stayed where he was.

Very slowly, Rhianna rose to her feet, putting the book down. The old man tensed, but didn't move. Step by step she moved towards him, talking gently, as if to a frightened animal. "And you must be cold, too, poor old fellow, here in this damp. Wouldn't you rather be warm and dry? What on earth made you hide down here? Whatever you did, it can't have been as bad as all that, and it's been long forgotten now."

He shuddered again, and then to her surprise he answered, after a fashion. "Didn't want to. They made me."

His voice was clear and cracked at the same time, like a child's and not like a child's. Rhianna moved a slow step nearer, talking gently. "Well, it wasn't your fault, then. You're not to blame. What did they make you do?"

He blinked up at her. "Talk to things. Hard things, cold things. But I ran away and hid. They couldn't find me. I bent the bars. They didn't think of that."

"That was clever of you. You didn't want to do what they wanted, so you ran away."

He nodded, pleased. She had understood him. "And hid. I hid. Long time."

"A very long time." She had approached within two steps. He shrank away, but she sank slowly down, kneeling, hands in her lap. "Your leg hurts, I'm sure. It looks very sore."

It was a long ragged cut across his shin and into his calf, deep and with bruised edges. He must have fallen against something, a sharp bit of metal, perhaps the edge of a stone. It looked angry, and it was still slowly weeping. He looked down, as if surprised at it. "Hurts, yes." He rubbed at it, and sucked his breath in. "Hurts," he said again, helplessly.

Very gently, Rhianna reached out a hand. The ankle was swollen, too. He'd turned it, probably in the same accident. A fall for sure, she thought. "It needs to be cleaned and bound up," she said, thinking aloud. "I can get some clean water, and warm it on the fire in the library. Then I can bathe that cut, and there's some healing herbs in Mother's medicine box. And Magister Northstar really ought to have a look at it. He knows healing magic."

But at the word *Magister*, the old man shied away violently and then he scrabbled backwards towards the wall, looking like a spider with his spindly limbs and tattered clothes. "No! No magic! No magisters! They made me. Ran away and hid, I did. Bars did what I told them, and I hid. Couldn't find me."

Rhianna stayed kneeling, and dropped her shoulders even lower. Some instinct was guiding her, telling her what to say. "No, all right." Her voice was gentle. "No magisters. Only me, if that is what you want. Only me. I'll wash that cut for you, and clean you up, and bind it. You want it to feel better, don't you? I promise, no magisters, no magic. But let me make it better."

He stared at her, fearful. "No magisters, no long-robes?"

She shook her head. "No. I promise. Only me. It hurts, doesn't it? Let me make it better."

He nodded, doubtfully. She rose to her feet, slowly. "I'll go and get some hot water and clean cloth, and some salve to put on that cut. You wait here. I won't be long."

When she returned, it was with a steaming basin and clean linen. As she had expected, the room was apparently empty again. But she knew how quietly he could move, and how many bolt-holes he had. She hadn't found all of them, not by a long chalk. She set the basin down and looked around. "Here I am again," she said. "Just me. Nobody else."

And there he was. Again she spent a good few minutes gently approaching, before kneeling with the basin and beginning the business of cleaning the cut. He flinched as she began to bathe the wound, in spite of her soothing voice. "Yes, I'm sorry, it hurts, doesn't it? It's a nasty cut, and beginning to get poisoned. It needs to be cleaned out. There, that's better. Let me wash it. How did you cut it?"

"I ran away," he said, open as a child.

"Yes, you said. You ran away and hid, didn't you?"

He nodded. "They made me. *They* made me, too. I didn't want to. But they caught me."

Rhianna was wringing out clean cloths in the hot water. She began gently bathing the cut, thinking about what he had just said. Something about it was puzzling her. "They caught you? But didn't you say they couldn't find you?"

"Not them, silly. *They* caught me. With barley sugar. Ouch!" He looked woeful as the cloth dabbed at the wound. "I like barley sugar," he added.

Barley sugar. She had found a new bag of barley sugar in the Underdark. If he had been caught with that as bait, it couldn't have been very long ago. But Magister Northstar had said the kitchen goblin had been raiding for forty years at least. Could there be *two* kitchen goblins? But he was so old . . .

And then it came to her. He was talking about two

different sets of people. Both had caught him, and he had hidden from both of them. Forty years apart.

She went on washing the cut. "Did they want the same thing?" she asked. There was something there, something she had half-guessed already.

He nodded. "The bars did what I told them," he said. "It's a trick."

She made her voice sound open, childlike. Like his. "Is it a good trick? I like clever tricks."

He smiled. "It's my best trick. Look."

He held out his open hand. Something lay across his palm. It was a heavy iron nail, handmade, square in section, almost as long as his hand was wide. Its point was blunt — probably he'd been using it to scrape mortar away from between stones to make peepholes. Otherwise it was just as it had been when he'd pulled it out of some board or other. Rhianna glanced at it, still wondering what he had meant about bars doing as he told them.

But a moment later she stopped wondering, because she knew what he had meant. The Wild Magic flared up like a flame. The nail began to bend. Just lying there, the head and point started to curve around towards each other, as if the nail were just a piece of string. Rhianna flicked a glance at the old man's face. He was smiling a little, and his eyes were intent. Again she looked at the nail, shocked, struck dumb, as it bent right round into a circle. She had never seen anyone else do something like that. No spells, no chants, no rhymes. The skinny old man just watched the nail — the cold iron nail — and it bent to his will. Just as the bars of his prison cell had bent for him, long ago, and he had fled into the Underdark. No, she had never seen anyone else do such a thing. But she had seen it done.

She had seen it done because she had done it herself. Cold iron had obeyed her will. It had obeyed her magic — the Wild Magic. The Wild Magic that she could taste on the air, the Wild Magic that the old man was using.

She became aware that he was watching her, and she pulled her eyes away from the iron nail that had become a ring of metal. She made herself smile. "That's a good trick," she said, and he smiled back at her. "But you mustn't do what they want you to with sharp things. That will get other people cut, just like this." He nodded, serious, like a child.

The cut was cleaned and washed out. She bandaged it with her mother's own ointment, knowing that would draw the poison, and then she began on the ankle. It, too, was swollen and bruised-looking. "You've twisted this badly," she said.

He nodded. "Hurts," he said.

"Well, it won't hurt so much if I bind it up close," she replied, and used broad strips of cloth to do that. "There.

That's better, isn't it?" He nodded, a little dubiously. She went on: "But I have to come back every day to change the dressing. You'll be here, won't you?"

"Another story?" he asked eagerly.

She almost laughed. "Another story," she agreed. "But only if you let me tend that leg. Otherwise it might turn bad."

He looked down at it, as if he'd forgotten about it already. "Doesn't hurt now," he said.

"It will, though, if it's not looked after. And there's one more thing." He tensed, suddenly wary. "No, don't worry. I'm not going to make you do anything. But tell me about these people who wanted you to talk to the iron. . . ."

CHAPTER 9

Later, Rhianna was talking with her master in his study. "I'm not sure I understand him, Magister. He runs things together in his mind, mixing what happened yesterday with what happened years and years ago. But I think it's plain enough who bespelled that sword. The question is, what made him do it?"

"Better you should ask *who* made him. You said he was frightened of wizards," said Northstar, and his eyes were full of anger and grief, both at once.

Rhianna shook her head. "I can't sort out who he's talking about, Magister. I don't know whether it was a wizard that frightened him not long ago, or whether it was more than forty years back."

"Well, we do know he bespelled that fiery sword not long ago. *Someone* frightened him into doing it."

"I . . ." But Rhianna never finished saying what she was going to say.

There was a rush of feet up the corridor outside and an urgent clamor of voices in the outer office. Then the door burst open without a knock. Magister Northstar looked up, his face thunderous, but he had no time to say anything, either.

Master Longacre, the Queen's Chamberlain, burst in. He was panting, and his face, for once, did not show polite deference. It was hard and urgent, and so was his voice. "Magister. The Queen commands your presence atop the King's Tower at once. A dragon is coming!"

Rhianna climbed the stairs at a run. This was the third or fourth flight, and her legs were starting to hurt. If her legs were sore, she couldn't think what it must be like for Magister Northstar, just ahead of her, but he climbed grimly on, going just as fast.

The stairs were a spiral winding up and up. This was the King's Tower, the oldest part of the Palace. It was built of thick stone, cold even now, with only slits for windows on landings that they rushed past. Archers stood by those slits, faces pale in the gloom, peering out. They knew how useless their arrows would be against the armor of a dragon, but still they stood their posts and prepared to resist.

At the top of the last twist of the stairs there was a square hole. They climbed up through it and emerged on the top of the tower, the highest and strongest in the Castle.

For a moment, Rhianna felt giddy with the height and the haste, gulping as she looked rapidly about her. From here, the whole of the Castle and the city could be seen spread out like a map, the roofs of the houses clustered under the grim walls like chicks under a hen. Ships like toys lay in the harbor far below, and all around the fretted blue sea rolled under the vast vault of the sky.

They stood on the flat stone roof. Other wizards stood around, some chattering and pointing, others staring. There was only a breastwork of battlement around them. Beyond that, over the bright sun-dazzle of the sea, two or three hundred paces off, a dragon flew.

How easy it is to say that, Rhianna thought, watching. *A dragon flew*. Simple words, really. But the trouble is that the words can give no idea of how it is. How can words tell you it? The air carried it as a man might carry something precious. It sparkled like gems, the sun striking gleams from it. Every scale shimmered in a dozen different colors — red-gold, emerald, sapphire, plum-purple. And yet saying that made it sound like a brightly painted toy, and said nothing of its grace. If you spoke of that, you would lose sight of the terrible power that lay under its smooth, easy flight. The dragon flew as though it caressed the air; but it was as large as one of the ships in the harbor below. And still you might think it beautiful and fragile, like colored glass, and forget that it was almost impossible to hurt, proof against all ordinary weapons and all but the strongest magics, steel-hard and tough beyond belief.

Rhianna had seen a dragon flying, once. Few people had seen so much. And yet, it was as if the sight was as new to her as to the gaping wizards that stood round about. It was not something you could ever get used to.

Magister Northstar rapped his staff sharply on the stone to get their attention. Faces turned towards him, excited chatter dying down. Rhianna recognized some of the faces. These wizards were in their everyday working clothes, but they were the same people as she had met on the dock that first day. They were the Masters of Wizardly College.

Northstar spoke rapidly. "Water-spells, if you please, colleagues. Better still, ice and snow to cool it off. Fire will only feed it. Master Hand, will you choose seven master wizards to form a Circle of Protection? Oh, and someone had better begin a repelling chant — I think Maulgram's Greater would be best. Who knows it?"

Rhianna was peering across the airy spaces at the dragon as it rode the wind. She suddenly narrowed her eyes, ran to the battlement, and leaned over, shading her eyes with her palm. The dragon drifted a little nearer, its enormous wings shifting to the updraft from the headland, soaring a little like a great seabird. She squinted, and then she pointed.

"Magister," she called, and her voice rose over the hubbub of the crowd. "Magister — the dragon — I think I know him."

Northstar was leaning his head towards Lord Odderer as the two conferred, preparing their most powerful magics. Now both of them swung around and stared out over the battlements.

Northstar's eyes narrowed and he shaded his eyes against the sun. At that moment, the dragon breathed. For a moment, it was as if the high summer sun had dimmed. Fire gushed from the mighty jaws, a long plume of flame, red at the edge, a violet-blue at the center that hurt the eyes. The wizards gasped. Some flinched; others began to chant. Magic sprang up; colored trails of misty ice glittered in the air.

The deadly flame had been sent aside. It touched no part of the town or the tower. The dragon's great wings bore it no nearer. It continued to soar above them like a mighty seabird, caressed by the winds that bore it. It stared at them, and made no move towards them.

"I think Rhianna is right," said Northstar. "This is the dragon that we turned away from Smallhaven village last year. There are not so many dragons, you know. And if it is that one, then he has kept his word. He did not return there."

Odderer shook his head. "No. Worse. He has come here instead."

"But not, I think, to burn and plunder. Look there! He breathes again, expending his flame harmlessly. He could have fired half the city by now. We were slow to respond. He has come to parley."

"No surrender to dragons," objected Odderer, and set his feet, looking mulish.

"No," said Northstar. "Certainly not. But perhaps he doesn't want us to surrender. Asking what he wants costs nothing, and we can always refuse." He stroked his beard. "Rhianna, I've a feeling he will hear you. Ask him to approach, and no tricks. If I see a sign of flame, the College will throw ice-spears that will pierce even his scales."

Rhianna nodded and leaned over the battlement. "Dragon," she called. "Come closer, but gently."

The dragon turned in flight. His wings flared, and he soared higher above them. His voice roared out, sounding in their ears like a great fire in the trees. "You will use no magic, and I will do no harm. Is it agreed?"

"It is agreed, dragon. Come."

The dragon slanted slowly down, and the wizards scattered to afford him space to alight. Alight he did, soft as a falling snowflake; but no snowflake ever glittered like that, and none put out a heat that could be felt ten paces away, as he did. He set his great clawed feet, neat as a cat on a wall, and Rhianna stared into slit-pupilled eyes that glowed with green fire, as old as the Palace — or perhaps even as old as the headland it stood on.

The dragon nodded at Northstar. "We have met before, you and I, great wizard," he said, in his voice that was like fire and like water on red-hot stone. "And you, too, wizardling, who will be greater still." His head was long and narrow and elegant, plumed like a dandy's ruff. "I greet you. But it is not you that I came to see."

Northstar cocked his head, and his eyes narrowed, but it was not he who answered. Another voice came, clear as a bell. "No. You came to speak with me, as is your right."

Gloriana, Queen of Avalon, stepped up from the stairs onto the flat old stones of the tower's roof. She was not now as Rhianna had seen her before. Straight and slim, yes, but now she wore a silk mantle embroidered with the Royal Arms of Avalon. The gemmed circlet of the Crown gleamed on her head, and she carried the Scepter of the Isles in her hand. Behind came her gaurds, with Duke Robert of Lamortin at their head, fully clad in armor and bearing the Royal Banner.

They would have put themselves between her and the dragon, but she held up a hand to motion them back, and then stepped forward. The wizards cleared a space between them, Rhianna moving aside with the rest.

"It is with me that you must speak, dragon," said the Queen. "Speak, then, and I will hear you."

The dragon stared down at her as she stood with head high, looking him in the eyes. "I see who you are," he said, "and it is indeed with you that I would speak. Tell me, Queen of Avalon, why have your people broken the Treaty, and begun to kill us?"

The Queen's chin rose. "None of my people has done as much," she said, and her voice was flat. "We have kept the Treaty, and killed no dragons."

The dragon's head drew back and his fanged mouth opened in anger. "Yet I saw you have not kept it, for I have seen the dead body of my mate pierced with a dozen wounds from a dragon-slayer's sword. Here is the sword, to give you the lie!"

It turned its snakelike neck around, and it drew a long sword from where it had been tucked inside the hollow of its foreleg. Rhianna tensed. She recognized it — it was twin to the one she had seen before. The Queen saw it, too, and she too froze rigid as the dragon held it in his mouth for a moment and then spat it with contempt on the stones at her feet. It clanged like a dropped pot, and broke into two pieces. Rhianna saw that the blade was bent and corroded. She felt the Wild Magic again, again mingled with sorrow and fear.

The Queen looked up from the sword as it lay before her feet. She glanced at Magister Northstar, who nodded, grimacing as if in bitter pain. He had seen Rhianna's face as she had felt the magic of the blade. Gloriana's eyes returned to the dragon. "This is not our doing," she said slowly. "We have not permitted this. If any of our people has done it, then I give my word that we will punish them as the Treaty requires."

The dragon hissed. "The Treaty requires more than that, Queen of Avalon. And we have kept it: peace, save for our ancient right to spell wrought-gold."

She nodded. "You say rightly, dragon. You have done so, and it does require more. Choose your hostage, then. I offer myself."

The dragon was silent a moment. Dragon faces cannot be read by humans, but still it seemed undecided. Then it spoke: "I will not take you. I think you are honest, and will try to find this killer-of-dragons. And your people will obey you. Humans are strange that way, and I will say that you, too, have abided by your word, until now. But the hostage must be one high in your councils and close to your heart."

The great slit-pupilled eyes traveled across the faces

of the throng. They paused for a moment on that of Duke Robert, but they moved again, seeking something else, something of meaning to a dragon. They came to the face of Magister Northstar, standing at the head of his College, his staff in his hand. "I will take your great wizard," said the dragon, and Rhianna gasped. "He will stand hostage, coming to no harm, until you find who has done this thing. But if you lie he will pay the price, and then the war will start again."

"It would be a war that your folk would lose, dragon," said Gloriana, and her voice was as cold and remote as a mountaintop.

The dragon hissed. It might have been dragon-laughter, but who could tell? "That is true, Queen of Avalon, for we are few and slow to breed, and there is no end to your numbers. You have magic, and in time you would bear us under and destroy us all. Well do we know it, and that is why we made the Treaty with your many-times grand-sire." Its great head reared up. "But how many of your folk would we take with us, in such a war? How many villages would burn? How much of this great city would lie in ashes? How many fields would be wasted, and how many of your people would starve? Many. Yes, we would lose in the end, but we would bring woe beyond reckoning to you. And I tell you, if we are to be hunted down whether we keep the peace or no, then we will not keep the peace." He turned his head. "Come, wizard."

Rhianna cried aloud, "No, Magister!" and would have started forward, but Northstar put out a hand, demanding obedience.

"Rhianna. Calm. The dragon is within his rights."

The Queen spoke. "He may choose a hostage, but I have already proposed myself as one, Antheus. He may not refuse that offer outright," she said.

Northstar bowed. "That is so, Your Majesty. Yet the dragon is right. You are needed here. I have every confidence that you will find this person." He turned to his apprentice. "Keep up your studies while I am away, Rhianna. Especially on the subject of string — and iron. Your friend Eriseth will no doubt help you there. Farewell for now."

He bowed to the Queen and walked with steady step up to the dragon. It lowered its head, and Northstar mounted astride the long scaly neck, his knees gripping the plates beside its spine, his heels locked into the hollow of its collarbones. It reared up again, and its rider was suddenly two men's height in the air.

"Farewell," it said. "He will come to no harm, unless another of my folk dies. When you have found and punished this dragon-slayer, send to me and you will have your Magister back again, with not a hair on his head singed. But should another be killed, then he dies and it is war."

The Queen said nothing, but stood straight as her guardsmen, face carved of stone. The dragon's wings unfurled, more enormous than the sails of a great ship. As they watched, it gathered its haunches under it, and then it leapt like a cat over the battlements, plunging in a long swoop that carried it far towards the rocks at the base of the headland far below, and then curving up, up, as the great wings bore it over the glittering sea. Northstar clung to its scales like a rider to a horse. The wings beat, flashing out like oars, and its speed was so great that it was gone in moments — nothing but a gleam in the sunlight, dragon and rider lost to sight.

Rhianna stood watching after him, and her face was grim. String, was it? Well, she had a string to follow, and the sooner she reached its end the better.

CHAPTER 10

Loys Wildwood was dressed in patched breeches and an old tunic that he had carefully stained with wine. He sat at a table facing the door — on his own, for even in a tavern like this one few were willing to disturb a man so large and strong. He nursed a mug of ale, sometimes spilling a little of it on the wooden floor, where it would lie unnoticed among the rest of the litter. His eyes stayed on the door.

A man would walk through that door soon. Garbutt was very loose in most ways, but he was as regular as a clock about going to the tavern in the evening. One of the ways in which he was loose was how much he talked when the drink was in him. Another was in his choice of who he talked to. He'd talk to anybody who'd buy him a drink. You hardly needed to ask questions at all, and sooner or later he'd tell you everything he knew.

Not that Garbutt knew much, thought Loys. Mainly

that life had been very unfair to him, and that nobody understood him, and that he had a dry throat. But he did know that he had made a sword for someone who knew nothing at all about swords. In fact, he'd made two. Perhaps this time he'd remember a little more about the man he'd cheated so cleverly. Perhaps he'd tell his old friend Loys all about it.

The tavern door opened. A man staggered in.

Mr. Wildwood let a beaming smile spread all over his face, and he waved for another mug of strong ale. The server, who was a small young girl with dark-honey hair, brought a pair of quart-pots on a tray. They were heavy, and she was slight and slim, but still she used surprisingly little effort in lifting them.

In her room in the Palace, Rhianna Wildwood prepared to go to sleep. She had kissed her mother good night, and she climbed into the wide, soft bed. Yet she was expecting to be wakeful, for she was worried.

That was for three separate reasons. She was worried about her father and Eriseth, who were late, and about Magister Northstar, who was the hostage of the dragons. But mainly she was worried about the old man in the Underdark, whom she had not seen that day. She had taken a storybook down to the room below the College scullery, but he had not come. She waited, but still he had not. Was he lying hurt somewhere? She knew that there were dangerous places down there, just as the Chamberlain had said, and the old man had been hurt before. His leg was better now, but still . . .

Odd, she thought, *I'm actually worried more about him than about Father and Eris.* Rhianna wondered if that was wrong of her — after all, you should care most for your own folk. But Father and Eris were rather good at looking after themselves, and they had each other. The old man had nobody to care for him. Nobody but Rhianna herself. She watched the darkness and worried, listening to the sounds of the Palace.

The Palace was full of faint noises, even at night. The corridors and passageways were never quite empty — someone was always running some errand or other, and the Guards paced the outer walls, calling the hours. The wind stirred in the corners and the eaves. The fountain played in the court outside, the old floors and roof beams creaked, and a faint hubbub from the city could be heard. Mother said that Avalon never slept. After a week here, Rhianna was prepared to believe it.

So it was that she took no notice of the faint creak and click. Perhaps she was already drifting into sleep without knowing it. But a moment later, she was wide-awake again. It wasn't the noises that had woken her, though. It was the Wild Magic. It was loose in her room, and she could feel it.

She sat up in bed with a gasp. And there was the old man, holding his hands out, palms towards her, looking frightened. He saw that she was awake, and he jigged from one foot to another, making shooshing noises. Rhianna stared at him. He had been crying, she saw, crying like a small child, and he was even now using his long white hair to wipe his face. His eyes were wild with fright.

"What's the matter, oh, dear, what's wrong?" she asked, and as she said it, she thought that it was how her own mother had asked about tears when she was little. The old man might have seen that, for it made a difference. His face still worked, but he seemed to calm.

Then he shook his head, putting a finger to his lips. He pointed. Rhianna looked, and her mouth opened. There, by the wall, was a trapdoor in the floor that she had never known was there. He had known a way into her room all along. And now he was beckoning, asking her to come with him. He was wild-eyed, too — frantic, jigging from foot to foot, urgent for her to follow him.

She glanced at the door. In her parents' bedroom her mother was doubtless lying awake, too, worrying. But the old man might have read her thoughts. He shook his head, and scampered backwards in the direction of his entrance, like a mouse retreating towards its hole. He would trust only her. Well, who else did he have to trust?

She slid out of bed, pulling on her slippers and a shawl. He was already dropping through the trapdoor, looking behind to make sure she was following. He had turned himself about and was walking down backwards. It was a ladder.

Rhianna picked up her lamp — a night-light, turned right down. She followed.

The ladder had been made out of odd bits of timber pegged and tied together. It was narrow, and the space she climbed into was dark, the sides rough and unfinished. An old chimney, perhaps, for there was soot in the crevices. It ran in the thickness of the wall, down, down. Rhianna was hampered by her shawl and her lamp. By the time she reached the end, the old man was out of sight.

At the bottom there was only a bare square of old bricks, anyway. Rhianna raised her lamp and saw that it had been a fireplace once, but the arch had been bricked up. A rough opening, just high enough to crawl through, was the only way on, and the old man must have gone that way. Sighing, she got down on her hands and knees to follow.

It was a crawl of perhaps twenty paces, sloping sharply down over rough stones and earth. Rhianna had to push the light ahead of her, and she knew she was getting her nightdress all dirty. Mother would not be pleased about this; but not for a moment did Rhianna think about turning back. It was dirty already, and clearly the old man needed her.

She came to a wider, higher space. High enough to stand up. She did so, and the lamp was suddenly not bright enough.

It was a hall, like the one just after the library, but she had never seen this one before. Again the walls were painted with stiff figures in shades of red, brown, and black, men and women and animals — cattle and sheep being led, fowls being carried. The figures were all looking towards the far wall, and there a painted man in a robe stood with his hands upraised. In one of those hands was a long, pointed knife. Beside him a doorway loomed, black in the shadows.

Rhianna tried to get her bearings. The chimney-shaft had led straight down, and the crawlway roughly towards the library. This must connect to the other painted rooms, somehow. How, she didn't know.

But there was no time for exploring. There was the old man, standing still. His head was on one side, and he was listening hard. Rhianna frowned and listened, too. She wished Eris were here. Eris would have heard whatever it was.

But so could she, after a bit. It was voices. Men's voices, in the distance, but echoing and getting closer.

"They're coming. Hide," whispered the old man.

They were the first words he'd said. Rhianna didn't question them. She looked around quickly. The room was bare and empty, but behind her, by the crawl space from which she had emerged, a flat piece of stone lay on the floor. It could clearly be fitted into the opening to hide it, and Rhianna retreated into the crawlway and hid behind it. She blew out her lantern, and the dark fell with a drop she almost felt. She crouched in the inky blackness, shaking her head.

Now that she had a moment, she began to wonder why she had obeyed the old man so quickly. Wizards have a way of making you listen, though, and there was no doubt that this was a Wild Mage, like Rhianna herself — one who had had a lifetime to practice. All the same, she thought that perhaps she shouldn't have been so easily carried along.

She was about to push the stone aside and come out again when light showed around the edges of it. At the same time, the words that the voices were saying became clear, and those words made Rhianna stop moving altogether.

". . . should have known that he could get loose. What's chains to someone who can bespell iron?"

The other voice was also a man's, lighter and cross. "Well, what else could I do? I can't be down here all the time. My absence would be noticed. He won't go far. It was you who were supposed to be watching him."

"I've got to sleep sometime, haven't I? I wish I could have gone with you. But I daren't be seen above. I'm not supposed to be in Avalon at all. I'd run into somebody I know, and that would lead to awkward questions."

"I can't help that. You were the one who got yourself into the Queen's bad books, and you chose a very bad time to do it. With your gear having to be handed in to the armory I had nothing to use."

"So you were cheated again. You bought another piece of useless rubbish."

"It did what it was meant to, didn't it? Am I an expert on swords? That was supposed to be *your* department."

"Pah! It nearly got me killed, dragon-slaying blade or not. I had to leave it in the dragon."

"So I saw. Another bungle. Now the Queen will never rest until she finds who did it."

"Well. I hope you learned something and found a better blade to use. Then perhaps we can allow the Queen to rest. Permanently, I trust. Oof, this is narrow. You're sure he's ahead?"

"Yes. He's powerful in a cracked sort of way, but he

knows little formal magic. I took the precaution of casting Tana's Tracker on him when he was asleep. It's a trifling spell, and he won't notice it, but it leaves a trail I can follow. He daren't go out. Ah. He's in here. I hadn't seen this bit before, though."

Rhianna found that she could peep around the edge of the stone. The room beyond suddenly blazed in cold white light.

Two figures emerged from the doorway.

Rhianna gasped. The first of them was Master Odderer, the Registrar of Wizardly College. He was robed, and his staff was in his hand. Its top burned with a brilliant white light, the wizard's light. He looked sternly down at the old man, who cowered and shrank into himself.

"Zosimus," said Master Odderer. "You promised that you wouldn't run away again." His voice was meant to sound kindly, but it was ice at the core.

The old man looked up at him, shaking. "You chained me," he quavered, "but she told me stories."

The other man, the one behind, spoke. "She? Who's this *she?*"

Odderer shook his head. "How should I know? His mother, maybe. He's addled. Although . . . his leg was bandaged neatly. He might be talking about . . ."

"It doesn't matter now. Make him do the sword."

"Gently, Captain, gently. The working has to be right. He has to do it properly. That's why you need me, to make sure he does."

And with that, Rhianna recognized the other man. It was Lysandus of Redhill, captain of the Queen's Guard. She gasped again.

Lysandus spoke. "And I will continue to need you, Odderer. Wizardly College will need a new Chancellor, just as Avalon will need a new king. Gloriana will be one of the first to fall in the Dragon War — such a shame, though she was a failure as a queen. But who to succeed her other than the dragon-slayer, the one who will lead us to victory? So let's have that sword." The Captain's eyes glittered in the hard bright light. His hands opened and clenched, as though the Crown was in their grasp already.

Odderer smiled. "Very well. A proper dragon-slaying blade. This is a far better sword — I just took delivery of it this evening — I paid extra for the overtime. It was made by a proper workshop, in spite of the risk that the smith would recognize it later." Master Odderer drew a sword from beneath his outer robe. It was plainer by far than the other two, but looked serviceable.

The Captain took the sword and inspected it, looking approving. Master Odderer held his hand out to get it back again, but the soldier held on to it. "Wait," he said.

"I don't see why the spell on the blade shouldn't be stronger yet. Dragons are not the only thing a king might need to fight."

Odderer frowned. "Don't be too greedy, Lysandus. There's the story of the frog who blew himself up until he burst. I'm not sure that I want to put an all-conquering sword in your hands."

"Don't you want to command all the wizards of the world? You will, you know. After I conquer."

Odderer did not answer directly. He gestured at the old man. "Zosimus can't bespell it from there, anyway. Let him hold it, and I'll instruct him."

The old man shrank away, but the Captain pushed the sword at him. "Tell him to make it infallible," ordered Lysandus. "Tell him to make sure it always deals a deadly stroke."

Odderer shook his head. "Spells like that go awry. You have to be exact." But he turned to the cowering old man. "Zosimus. Make the blade harder and sharper and tougher. Make it to cut through a dragon's scales, like the last one."

Zosimus backed away, his hands behind him, averting his head from the sword held out by Lysandus. "I don't want to. She said not to, she said it would cut people . . ."

The wizard tried to sound reasonable: "Zosimus, you must . . ."

"No, no, no!" Each word was louder than the last, like a toddler.

Odderer stamped his foot. "What nonsense is this? Zosimus, do as you're told."

But Lysandus merely grunted, and pushed in front. "Listen, you addled old coot, do as we say, or else I'll drag you out of here and put you in a cage and we'll cut you open to get your magic out." He grabbed him by the scruff, thrusting the sword at him. "Do it!" His voice rose to a roar, and Zosimus burst into terrified tears, sobbing, wailing, wiping his eyes with his long white hair.

Rhianna could stand no more. Pure rage flooded through her. Cheats! Bullies! How dare they? In a moment she had thrust the stone aside and was scrambling out. She had no idea what she was going to do, and for a moment she could only stand, blinking in the hard light, shaking with anger. And she had to think . . . she had to take off the jewel that drained her magic. She should have done that already. She clutched at it and dragged it over her head, to let it drop on the floor at her feet. The Wild Magic poured in, staggering her, urgent to be released. She had to take a moment to control it.

That gave Odderer time. He recovered and recognized her. "Northstar's pupil! The Wild Mage!" And then his staff leapt up. He made a complicated gesture and called a word.

Rhianna felt the sudden shock of magic. She knew the spell — she had seen her own master use it, once. It was a silencer. She could not speak now, unless she were strong enough to break the spell. It was the usual first move of a wizard's duel, to silence the other so that no magic word or chant could be used. Clever wizards could tie opponents hand and foot like a spider with a fly, and smile while they struggled to break out and make their own magic, the magic of sign and word.

Odderer saw her stand silent, and he smiled. Perhaps this Wild Mage was not as clever as she thought. For all her power, she was unskilled and unpracticed. He prepared his next spell, and Rhianna could only watch him silently, steeling herself for the shock as he wove word and hand together.

CHAPTER 11

". . . *etwas Naareo!*" Rhianna had never heard of this spell, but she could see the effect. Over in the corner, out of the light, something was making itself out of the darkness. It was a shadow taking on solid form, a lumbering squat lump. Limbs grew from a vague blob of a body, with the head a doughy mass on top. Glittering specks, a dozen of them, were its eyes. It opened a wide mouth, and the mouth was filled with teeth like spikes of black ice.

Odderer gestured with his staff, and it snuffled like a hound. Its little eyes shifted and blinked. It stirred, then took a step on blunt feet that rolled like clouds. Another. Another. And each one was towards Rhianna.

Zosimus called out in fear. Lysandus pushed the sword at him, but he wailed and wriggled, and the soldier shook him like a rat.

While they struggled, Rhianna watched the shadow-thing advance across the dim room. It was made of darkness; but she had been reading about light. It was light that she called on, for where there is light there can be no darkness.

In the air around her, a golden glow began to form. It brightened as she called on the Wild Magic, opening like a flower, warm and welcoming against the cold gray of the shadow-creature. She had no need for words or staff or gesture. The Wild Magic poured out, glad to be released, sharpened by her anger, and yet she had it controlled, as a rider controls a spirited horse.

The golden glow sharpened, as if being focused by a glass. It brightened, and then it was a shaft of brilliant light. In a moment, it had become a spear tipped with shining white-gold like the heart of a furnace. Rhianna stood silent, making no movement, and yet it leapt the gap to the shuffling shadow-thing in an instant.

For just a moment, it was as if a golden leopard was pouncing. Suddenly the shadow was itself harder edged, lined in light. A wail escaped it. Then its form crumpled and diminished under the onslaught, and it fell into itself, shrank away and was lost. A shower of golden sparkles rippled in the air where it had been, but it was gone.

Odderer gasped. The girl had made no spells, said no chants. He had silenced her; she should be helpless, yet she had made magic of her own to strike his down. "Lysandus!" he called. "Help me!"

"Aye, I will that," snarled the soldier. "But I'll have the sword first." He shook the sobbing Zosimus again. "Hear me, old fool! Do as I say, or I'll use the sword on you, to find out where your spells come from. Give me a sword that protects me against all others, and never misses its deadly stroke." He held the sword before the old man's terrified eyes. "Give it me!"

Rhianna would have shouted in anger, but she could not. She gathered up her light again, and again it became a spear. She pointed it at the wizard, and sent it flashing across the space between them.

Odderer was sweating freely in the cold room. He called a word, and a shadow sprang up before him, a flat black plate like a shield. The light-spear crashed into it with a rending snap, and again all that was left was a drifting curtain of golden sparkles in the air.

"No, no," wailed Zosimus. "You'll hurt us with it."

Lysandus smiled. Odderer was panting. "Hurry, for heaven's sake," the wizard called. "She's too strong. I can only hold her off for a while. Get to her before it's too late!"

His hands were weaving patterns in the air. Dark swirls seemed to pour out of them.

Lysandus was speaking to Zosimus. "I won't hurt her, Zosimus. Nor you, either, if you give me the sword. Promise." His voice was calm, but he held on to the old man's scruff like a terrier. "But give me the sword, or I'll go straight to her and cut her, and make you watch."

Zosimus wiped his arm across his eyes. "Promise you won't hurt us!" he wailed.

The silence spell still held Rhianna. She struggled against it, and it began to unravel. She felt its bonds weakening, but at the same time the swirling darkness around Odderer's hands took on shape. It became a black floating octopus, drifting in the air as if it were the depths of the sea, a mass of twisting legs around a cloudy head. A dark sparkle within the head became a snapping parrot beak.

But golden light was drifting down on it in falling sparkles, and each spark ate away a little of its shadowy substance, dissolving it like salt left out in the rain. It thinned out and became less.

"Hurry!" shouted Odderer. The floating octopus flailed in the air, and then spat an inky cloud. And still the golden sparkles fell, melting it away.

"A moment, wizard." Lysandus was holding out the sword to the old man. "Remember, old man, it must protect me from all others, and it must never miss giving a deadly stroke." Zosimus nodded, and Rhianna could only look on, horrified, still held silent.

"And you won't hurt us?" said the old man.

"Hurt you? No, no, of course not." The Captain's voice was confident. "Hurry."

The wrinkled old hands were on the blade, stroking it like a cat, probing it as if for secrets. Zosimus bowed his head, and then tensed. He shuddered once, and let out a pent-up breath.

Odderer had used the moment while Rhianna struggled against the silence-spell. He shaped darkness into a cloud over the struggling shadow-beast, sheltering it from the raining golden fire, and it gained mass and shape again. Rhianna had to call again, and the Wild Magic became a circle of light like a pinwheel. She sent it scything across the room to slice into the shadow-stuff. The writhing tentacles folded up against the head, like a struck spider. It released more ink, and then it disappeared into a hole in the air, like a squid hurling itself away from an attacker.

"Help me, now!" shouted Odderer. His voice sounded ragged, desperate.

Zosimus had released the sword. He looked up shakily, and the Captain brandished the blade high. "Help you, wizard?" Lysandus snarled, and in the snarl was triumph. "Are you so weak that you cannot defeat a girl-child? You are no further use to me, then, and anyway you know too much."

The sword slashed down. Odderer seemed to leap

aside, but the blade followed him, without effort from the hand holding it. Sure as a hawk's stoop it was, and a moment later Odderer fell dead.

"Ha!" Lysandus's voice was a great roar of glee. "You didn't cheat me, old man. It turned on him like a hound on a rabbit. A deadly stroke indeed. For that, I might let you live."

Rhianna, sick to her soul, hurled her Wild Magic against the spell holding her silent. It burst asunder. She could speak again.

"Murderer!" she cried out in horror.

Lysandus only smiled. "No murder to slay a traitor, and Odderer was a natural one. He would have betrayed me just as quickly." His eyes narrowed. "But a king cannot risk such an accusation. Pity. Clearly, you're a powerful magic-worker. I could have used you, but you'll never be reliable."

He had been sauntering forward as he spoke. Now he rushed at her. Rhianna had a moment to hurl a spear of golden light. It flashed across the gap between them, but the sword snapped up in the soldier's hand, and it met the light edge-on. It flared like the sun, drinking down the power of the magic, and Lysandus shouted aloud. "Again you are of use, old man. I believe I *shall* let you live!"

Rhianna tried to leap aside. Lysandus aimed no stroke, but his shoulder cannoned into her, and she was knocked sprawling, stunned as her head struck the floor. He hardly staggered, standing over her. As she crashed down, the sword swung up.

"Hold still, missy," he grunted, "and you'll hardly feel a thing . . . what!"

The last word was a startled shout, over the thrum of a bowstring. The sword had twisted in his hands, turning suddenly, wrenching him around. A sharp clang, and a long arrow splintered off the blade as the sword cut it out of the air.

For a moment they held thus, Rhianna stunned on the floor, the Captain standing over her, staring behind — and Eriseth Arwensgrove at the door, grabbing another arrow from her quiver and drawing her bow again. Again she shot, and again the sword met the flying arrow, moving faster than the eye could follow, cutting it out of the air to skitter across the floor.

Lysandus had been wide-eyed with surprise. Now he laughed. "An archer, now!" Eriseth seemed surprised herself. She lowered the bow for a moment, blinking. The Captain flourished the sword. "But your arrows are no more use than her spells. You can't hurt me while I hold this." Eriseth groped for another arrow. He laughed again. "Aye, go ahead and lose. While you do that, I'll just finish this one, and then I'll come for you."

Eriseth drew, but she held her shaft. "Too late, traitor," she called. "It'll do you no good to murder again. My master has gone for the Queen's Guard. They'll take you and wrestle that sword from you, if they must."

The smile vanished from the Captain's face. "Then I must go find another dragon to slay. Once the war starts, the Queen will have little time to worry about me, and there'll be plenty of work for a dragon-slayer. I'll be a king yet!"

Eriseth gasped, and her face hardened into rage. She shot. Again the sword flashed out and caught the arrow on the wing, cutting it to the floor. "Fool!" snarled Lysandus. "Now your friend is dead."

He raised the sword again, and sent it slicing down. Zosimus cried out, "You promised!"

Perhaps there was not only despair in that wail. Perhaps there was something else as well. Lysandus made no reply, of course. His face merely showed his pleasure. And then it showed amazement.

For the sword swung in an impossible-looking curve as it flashed down. Rhianna closed her eyes, but she felt only the wind of the blade. And then heard an ugly thud and a gasp.

She opened her eyes again. Lysandus still stood over her, hands on the hilt of the sword. His eyes were blazing with amazement and surprise. He tugged on the hilt, and Rhianna, following the movement, saw with a sudden shock of horror that the blade was buried in the side of his chest. He tugged again, puzzled and shocked at what had happened to him. Then his eyes rolled up in his head, his mouth dropped open, and his knees began to sag.

She scrambled away, pushing back across the stones. He tottered, then he fell straight backwards. A clatter, and his hands were jerked away from the sword hilt as he hit the floor, but the blade stayed where it was. His mouth moved, as if he would say something, but it was only a sigh, and then he relaxed.

Rhianna and Eriseth stared at each other, and at the old man. The darkness deepened as Rhianna's golden light faded, but none of them could rouse themselves to mend it. It had almost gone by the time the Queen's Guard burst in, with the Queen herself at their head. But even the Queen could not take precedence over Loys Wildwood. He ran ahead, took one look, and gathered both his girls in his arms. It was only then that they were able to cry.

CHAPTER 12

On the tower's flat roof, far above the silver-laced sea, Magister Northstar climbed stiffly down from the dragon's neck. He looked up and nodded, and the great head lowered in return.

"The sword will be broken into pieces," he said.

"Aye." That was the Queen. "And the pieces shall be thrown into the deepest sea. I give my word on it, and you may witness for yourself."

The dragon's voice was a roaring fire. "Well enough. Yet it will not bring back my mate. This must not happen again."

"No." Gloriana glanced at Rhianna, but she gave no other sign. "It must not. We have suffered, too, dragon. My people lie dead; two villages are ruins. We must work together to prevent it. Will you take a spellcaster, so that we may give warning if another would-be dragon-slayer should arise?"

The dragon seemed to consider, but perhaps it was surprise. "Work together?" it asked.

They were at supper, a few days later. "Lucky you turned up in time," said Northstar to Eriseth. "How did you manage it?"

Eriseth glanced at her master. Loys Wildwood shook his head. "It wasn't luck," he said. "Garbutt was angry with Odderer for refusing to be cheated a third time, and was happy to take my money to point him out when he came to take delivery of the third sword. Eris followed him, while I went to the Queen. Her Majesty was prepared to listen."

"Yes," said Eriseth. "If anything, our luck went sour then. He used the trapdoor in the Palace kitchen, but then the way into the room you were in had been hidden. It was through the bricked-up window in that old bathroom — some of the bricks had been loosened, and a crawlway made. It balked me for a moment, until I saw the loose mortar, and then I had to go back to lay a trail from the library entrance to guide the others, so I was late. But Zosimus had arranged it all neatly. Rhianna, you were never in danger, really. He'd fixed it."

Rhianna nodded. They watched Zosimus. The old man stared down at the table, then looked up again. "Bad man broke his promise," he said, and held out his plate for another slice of pudding. Mrs. Wildwood raised her eyebrows at him. "Please?" he asked, and she nodded and cut him one.

"Yes, he did," said Rhianna. "And you did exactly as the man told you, didn't you, Zosimus? A sword that protected him from *others,* and always dealt a deadly stroke. But you made it so it couldn't hurt me. And you did that first." She sighed. "You couldn't have known what Lysandus would do with it, could you?"

"Couldn't he?" asked Magister Northstar. "I don't know." He pushed his bowl back.

They watched Zosimus as he ate pudding with plenty of custard, making little smacking noises. He was clean, now, and perhaps not as gaunt as he had been. His hair and beard had been neatly trimmed, and he was clothed properly. Not that it stopped him from getting custard on his front.

"He's a Wild Mage, too, you know," said Eriseth. "What will happen to him?"

Magister Northstar sighed. "He'll be properly cared for here in the Palace. Her Majesty has seen fit to grant him a small pension, and his needs are simple." He caught his apprentice's glance. "I give my word that he will never be forced to work the Wild Magic for anyone, ever again. Indeed, we must keep his gift secret. The dragons distrust it. Yet they are willing to talk."

"So there will be peace."

"Yes. For now. But . . ." He looked across at his apprentice. ". . . too many people know that iron can be bespelled, now." Rhianna understood.

Northstar nodded. "Yes. We have given it out that Odderer discovered how to do it, and that the way was lost with him. But that might not be enough. Your talent is also known, Rhianna. Someone — King Hrothwil, for example — might put two and two together, eventually."

"And if he does, Magister?" Loys Wildwood had a sharp stare for the wizard.

Magister Northstar stared straight back. "Then we must be prepared to protect Rhianna. And the best way to do that is to make her able to protect herself. Already she has shown her power. Odderer was neither weakling nor fool, and she bested him." He laced his fingers together. "I think it is time for her real magical education to start. That was why I said she would be seeing Zosimus often. Here, in Avalon."

He sat and stared at them, and they stared back.

ABOUT THE AUTHOR

Dave Luckett writes in many genres, but his first loves are fantasy and science fiction. He has won many accolades for his work, including three Aurealis Awards.

Although he was born in New South Wales, Dave has lived for most of his life in Perth, Western Australia. A full-time writer, he is married with one son.

Ella. Snow. Rapunzel. Rose.
Four friends who wait for no prince.

from best-selling authors
Jane B. Mason and Sarah Hines Stephens

With her feet bare (those glass slippers don't fit), and her second-hand gown splattered with mud (thanks, evil stepsisters), Ella's first day of Princess School is off to a lousy start. Then she meets silly Snow, adventurous Rapunzel, and beautiful, sheltered Rose. Ella's new friends make Princess School bearable—even fun. But can they help Ella stand up to her horrible steps in time for the Coronation Ball?

SCHOLASTIC and associated logos are trademarks and/or registered trademarks of Scholastic Inc.

www.scholastic.com